Lady Rample Steps Out

Lady Rample Mysteries:
Book One

Shéa MacLeod

Lady Rample Steps Out

With gratitude to Dame Agatha Christie,
who inspired a young girl to follow her dreams.

Lady Rample Steps Out

Chapter 1

If Sir Eustace didn't stop yammering on about his adventures in Africa, there was bound to be a murder. His. And the authorities wouldn't have far to look to find the killer. "Sorry, officer, it was him or me. Self-defense and all that. I was bored out of my skull. You understand."

"There I was, face to face with the king of beasts, nothing on me but my pipe. What a to-do!" Sir Eustace gave a belly laugh, his monstrous, white sideburns—in defiance of all current modes of fashion—bobbled wildly. It might be 1932 London, but Sir Eustace was firmly entrenched in tales of the high planes of Africa sometime well before George V took the throne.

I took a sip of my highball and made a moue, disappointed. I am inordinately fond of highballs, being my cocktail of choice, but the ginger ale was altogether too spicy. It zinged up my nose making my sinuses itch. Anyone who knew anything about mixing beverages knew that ginger ale in a highball should be sweet and sparkly, not spicy. At least they hadn't used club soda, I suppose. I'd had it made that way once or twice. Vile.

Reluctantly, I set my glass down on the side table, not much caring if I left water rings on the polished, dark wood which smelled faintly of lemon and wax. After all, Sir Eustace deserved a little furniture destruction, boring me to tears as he was. Really, the man had probably spent all his time in Africa indoors. And I was certain he'd never faced down a lion, no matter what he claimed. I cast a longing glance at the dark amber liquid teasing me from within the cut-glass tumbler. It looked better than it tasted. Most unfortunate since I was in dire need of a drink—or several—if I were to survive Sir Eustace.

If only this unutterably dull affair had been scheduled a week earlier. I could have bowed out, thanks to the appropriate yearlong grieving period. Not that I had been grieving, to be perfectly frank. I'd actually been quite busy with business matters and visiting my newly inherited properties. It just gave me an excellent excuse to get out of ridiculous parties such as the one I was currently attending. Alas, the year was up, and I was forced back into society against my will. Not that I minded society for the most part. I like a good party as much as anyone else. The operative term being "good."

I stifled a yawn behind my white satin glove, not much caring if anyone saw. Maybe Sir Eustace would get a hint, unlikely as that was. The man was thick as a brick.

Once upon a time, I had the great good fortune to meet and marry Lord Rample, a gentleman quite senior to me in both age and rank. It had all been my Aunt Butty's doing, of course. The woman was an irrepressible matchmaker and thoroughly convinced that wealthy husbands were the way to go. Lord Rample had the great good fortune to be not only enormously wealthy, but without much in the way of heirs. She decided he was perfect. Not for her own husband number four, but for my husband number one.

The result had been a séance—Aunt Butty was obsessed with spiritualism regardless of it having fallen out of style—in which Queen Victoria's ghost had appeared and ordered him to marry me. Fortunately, Lord Rample had taken it in stride. He didn't marry me immediately, but he did ask me on a carriage ride in Hyde Park during which the horses bolted, forcing poor Lord Rample to play hero and take over the reins, bringing us to a safe stop. I'd have blamed Aunt Butty for arranging that, but I can't see how she could have done it seeing as she was in Cairo at the time.

In any case, Lord Rample had seemed quite sophisticated and heroic and eventually I'd agreed to marry him. Aunt Butty had been overjoyed.

When Lord Rample had the generosity to die a mere four years into our marriage, he had left me not only with the title of Lady Rample, but also with more money than God Himself would know what to do with. Only the country manor up in the wilds of North Yorkshire—still entailed under a ridiculous ancient British law—had gone to a distant cousin by the unfortunate moniker of Buck-toothed Binky (His real name was Alphonse, so you can see why he might prefer the moniker). Frankly, I had been glad to see the back of it. The place was drafty, in poor taste, and a bottomless money pit. I was quite satisfied with the London townhouse, a few properties abroad, and enough money to swim in.

A loud guffaw jerked my attention back into the room. What a lot of dull people! Every one of them had a title—some multiples. Most of them had money—though not as much as I did, which amused me no end since they tended to look down their collective aquiline noses at a mere vicar's daughter. And all of them were wrapped up entirely in the social mores necessary to maintain whatever status they clung to. Frankly, I was tired of it.

I slid a sideways look at a plump woman swathed in an unfortunate amount of peach satin. Lady Chatelain had been the first to dub me a "merry widow." Which was ridiculous. I had been rather fond of my elderly husband. He was a dear and often bought me nice presents and paid me lovely compliments and ushered me about proudly. I'd found no fault with him as a husband. I simply hadn't had any passion for him, nor he for me. We'd been more like affectionate roommates, which was precisely what each of us had wished when we got married. And thus, parading around in black felt...false. Felix—Lord Rample—would have detested it. So I had chosen dark colors such as plum and navy which both suited my complexion and spoke to mourning without being showy about it. I felt strongly that Felix would approve.

Now that a year had gone by, however, I had thrown off my widow's weeds and stepped out. Even the snobby *le beau monde* couldn't disapprove of that. Well, they could, but it would be churlish of them.

Sir Eustace, God love him, had launched into yet another dull tale, this time of his adventures in Constantinople. Istanbul, I guess they call it now. You'd think that tales of such a place would be exciting, thrilling, exotic. You would be incorrect. Sir Eustace had the ability to turn the most interesting story into a downright yawn. Too bad. I'd always wanted to travel. Perhaps now I would. Maybe I should buy a ticket on the Orient Express. Get out of London for a while. Have an adventure. Then I'd have my own tales with which to bore the aristocracy.

My name is Ophelia, Lady Rample. If you ask anyone in the room, they will tell you I drink too much, drive too fast, and have a tendency to be seen in the company of unsuitable men. If I were a lesser woman, I'd be ostracized from polite society. Not that it would be any loss, frankly. Polite society is ridiculously dull. However, seeing as how I am—as the Americans so cheerfully refer to it—*loaded*, I am forgiven a great multitude of sins and deemed an "original." Or sometimes the less kind term of "eccentric."

At last I could stand no more of Sir Eustace's prattering on. I quietly slipped from the stuffy drawing room and made as if to take advantage of the powder room. No need to offend my hostess. Lady Mary was a sweet woman and hardly to blame for her husband's distinct lack of talent in storytelling.

The corridor was empty save for a hideous wooden statue holding a spear, so instead of turning left for the powder room, I veered right toward Sir Eustace's study where I knew he kept an excellent scotch. Felix had told me about it once. The two of them used to hide out, drink, and smoke cigars together. I make it a habit to never forget the location of good booze.

The study was, fortunately, empty, with only a low fire burning in the grate. It was a manly sort of place redolent of leather and old books. The view of the street outside was blocked by heavy velvet curtains of an indistinct color—possibly blue or green. A massive and ill-advised painting of a hunt—overly decorated in blood—hung above the fireplace. Leather bound books sat untouched on shelves. Sir Eustace wasn't much of a reader, according to Felix. Much preferred shooting things.

A stunning art deco bar cabinet sat in one corner, wood gleaming softly in the firelight. I smiled to myself as I strode across the room, my heels silent on the thick carpet. I carefully opened the rich, walnut panels and eyed the copious bottles within. Sure enough, there was a vintage scotch that must have set Sir Eustace back a pretty penny.

I poured two fingers of the stuff into a crystal tumbler and eyed myself in the mirrored lid. My golden-brown locks, carefully waved by my maid, were still perfectly in place and my gray-green eyes were still neatly rimmed in smoky kohl. However, my raspberry lipstick could use a bit of attention. I touched it up a tad before shutting the bar. Hopefully, Sir Eustace wouldn't notice. Stealing a man's scotch was not the done thing.

I would have preferred ice—very un-British of me—but there wasn't any. Straight up would have to do. Drink in hand, I sauntered out into the hall and made my way to the back of the house and the veranda overlooking the garden overflowing with wisteria and hollyhocks. During the day, it would be a place of stunning beauty. Even at night, it wasn't without its charms. White lilacs glowed softly in the moonlight while the scent of narcissus perfumed the air. Mary had a way with plants. No doubt the garden was an escape from her dreary husband. Personally, I'd have drunk his scotch.

"I wondered where you'd got to." The voice was rich and rumbly, smooth as fresh churned butter and accompanied by the scent of cedar wood and sweet pipe tobacco.

I gave the new arrival a sidelong glance, marveling for perhaps the hundredth time at what a singularly handsome fellow he was. Not a hair out of place and every article of clothing just so. The modern-day Beau Brummel. Too bad I wasn't his type. Still, we had a jolly good time together. "Don't tell me you were enjoying the ramblings of Sir Eustace."

"Good lord, no." His tone was hearty. "It's a good deal Sir E keeps a well-stocked bar." He jiggled his own tumbler back and forth. He'd apparently come by his honestly as it held ice.

"Do you think we can get out of here? I'm afraid if I stay here another minute I shall do something drastic. Throw myself off the veranda, perhaps." It was all of a four-foot drop, the ground below soft from spring rains. The worst I'd do is end up with grass stains on my gown and a slightly damp posterior. Any additional mar to my reputation would only amuse me. I had better things to do with my life than worry about whether or not I was being gossiped about.

He chuckled. "We can't have that now, can we? Drink up. We'll find somewhere a little livelier."

Charles "Chaz" Raynott the Third was what one might term my best friend, if he were a woman. I wasn't sure it was the done thing to have a man best friend, but the done thing never stopped me from doing precisely as I pleased—boring soirees aside. He was also the perfect escort, being ridiculously good looking, perfectly manicured, and of the proper pedigree to boot. In fact, if I'd been in the market for a new husband, he'd likely have made an excellent one of those, as well. Except for one teeny factor: Chaz was what some would politely term "light on his feet." Seeing as how that was illegal— ridiculous nonsense, if you ask me—having a female friend to squire around kept him safe from wagging tongues, not to mention a prison sentence.

Of course, spending so much time together led to a few rumors. Frankly, none of them bothered me. Those that mattered knew the truth. Those that gossiped didn't matter. Wagging tongues were fine as long as they didn't wag the truth.

Chaz and I had been friends for years, ever since he was injured during the Great War and found himself under my dubious care. We'd both been impossibly young, but perhaps less naive than we should have been. We'd met again years later, and a strange friendship had been born. Felix had adored Chaz almost as much as I did, and Chaz's proclivities never seemed to bother him, though he didn't mention it, so perhaps he simply ignored reality for my sake.

One of the brilliant things about Chaz was that he always knew the most interesting people. Sometimes the places he took me to skirted decency, but they were never unsafe, and we always had a spiffing time.

I downed the scotch fast enough to make Felix wince—he was of the opinion that good scotch should be savored over a lengthy period of time and possibly a pipe—and left my tumbler sitting on the balustrade. "Where to, darling?"

Chaz grinned, flashing perfect white teeth. How he got his teeth so white, I'll never know. "Follow me, old bean. It's a surprise!"

We slipped past the open doors of the drawing room where Sir Eustace droned on. Easy enough. Convincing the maid to bring our outerwear without notifying her mistress, Lady Mary, was another matter, but Chaz was ready as always with a saucy wink, a smooth compliment, and a couple of clinking coins. In no time at all, I was wrapped in my mink stole, Chaz had on his wool overcoat, and we were climbing into his Bentley. Black and sleek, like his wardrobe.

The tires hummed against wet pavement. It had been raining for positively weeks. Well, days, anyway. Typical English spring weather. I was getting quite tired of it. Perhaps a trip to the south of France was in order. I could visit the villa in Nice. I did so love the French Riviera. Felix had taken me there shortly after we married. It was my first trip abroad, and I was smitten.

While most of my compatriots lounged on the beaches or on the deck of some yacht or other, I roamed the cobblestone streets and quaint little shops. I was determined to find the very best croissant in all of France. Or at least in the Riviera. That meant a trip to every patisserie between Marseille and Nice. Felix had never complained once, and we'd both put on half a stone.

The car drew up in front of a plain, brick building on the edge of Soho—West London's famed entertainment district. A neat, neon sign perched above a simple door. I squinted slightly against the rain streaking the window and made out the words in red lights: Astoria Club.

"You're taking me to a club?" An evening of boredom stretched in front of me, men smoking cigars, women nattering inanely. Yawn-worthy music picked out on a grand piano. "You should have left me at the mercy of Sir Eustace. It would have been kinder."

"This isn't any old club. Be a good sport."

I grimaced. Being a good sport usually got me into trouble where Chaz was concerned. Not that I minded. Trouble could be fun. Felix always said I had a nose for it. He wasn't entirely wrong.

Chaz gallantly wielded the umbrella while I extricated myself from the car. I clutched his arm as we darted toward the door of the club, rain drizzling around us in a fine mist.

The door opened on a blast of warm air, and we were ushered into a tiny vestibule by a red-jacketed doorman. He looked ridiculously young, cheeks still childishly chubby and not enough fuzz to make a proper moustache. A small, red fez perched jauntily at an angle on his baby-fine hair. "Welcome, sir. Madam."

The vestibule was carpeted in deep red to match the wallpaper, a counter to the right manned by a young woman with elegantly Marcel-waved platinum blonde hair and a mole above her upper lip. I wondered vaguely if it were real or painted on. She took our outerwear in exchange for a gold token which Chaz tucked away in the pocket of his tuxedo trousers.

The doorman bowed elegantly and opened a second door which opened on a set of stairs, dimly lit, leading down into Heaven knew where.

"Ready, old bean?" Chaz offered his arm again.

I took a deep breath and his arm. "Why not? In for a penny, in for a pound."

"That's the spirit!"

And down we went, into the belly of the beast.

Shéa MacLeod

Chapter 2

At the bottom of the stairs stood a forbidding set of double doors. They were thick oak wood, stained dark and bound in iron, like something out of a dungeon. The Tower of London, perhaps. With skeletons of little princes locked away behind them. Good lord, I was maudlin.

From the other side, I heard muffled music, but I couldn't quite make out the melody. A red-jacketed bouncer stood guard. He was less chubby and more muscular than the doorman, his handlebar moustache at odds with his shiny bald pate.

He opened the door for us, and out swirled the sweet wail of a saxophone along with a heady cloud of cigarette smoke tinged with something almost floral. A wide grin spread across my face and made my cheeks ache. I was instantly giddy. Not because of the smoke—I've never gotten the hang of it (filthy habit)—but because of the music.

"Jazz. You brought me to a jazz club."

"Best in the city," Chaz said, proud of himself. "Very hush-hush. Only those in the know, darling."

"Well, don't I feel the bee's knees." I chuckled, listening with delight, my toes already tapping to the beat. "The band is spiffing." As we moved inside the club, the doors swung shut behind us. I noted the inside of the doors were heavily padded and quilted in wine colored velvet, which explained why we hadn't heard the music outside.

The club wasn't terribly large. There were only about half a dozen small, round tables scattered about the edges of the dance floor where a handful of couples danced a lively Balboa, bodies pressed up against each other in a way that would have scandalized most of the attendees of Sir Eustace's party. Along the walls were padded booths—mostly occupied with canoodling couples—in the same wine velvet as the doors. In front of us was a raised dais where the band—dressed in black tails and ties—played with enthusiasm. To the right was a long marble bar, smoothly polished to a high gloss. It matched the ceiling from which dripped several small crystal chandeliers. Behind the bar, bottles glowed softly in the dim light.

A short, round man with a thin, black moustache and the most amazingly bushy eyebrows toddled over to us. He wore the same black tails and tie as the band, but his waistcoat was wine to match the upholstery, and he wore a white carnation in his lapel. He looked for all the world like a well-dressed penguin.

"Mr. Raynott, good of you to grace our humble halls once again." The little man beamed from ear-to-ear. He bowed to me. "Welcome, Madam. Please, follow me."

He waddled ahead of us to a corner booth set at the perfect angle for watching the band, while being out of the line of sight of the other patrons. Heavy, wine velvet drapes held back with gold tassels graced either end of the booth. I wasn't sure if they were for show, or if one could actually pull them closed for privacy. It seemed a little...obvious, if that was the case.

Once we were seated, a black-suited waiter appeared, as if by magic, to take our drinks order. Then he whisked away almost as abruptly as he'd arrived, leaving us to our own devices.

A candle flickered in the center of the table, accompanied by the smell of hot wax. It cast eerie shadows across Chaz's face, emphasizing the devilish in the handsome. I turned my attention to the band. I was astonished to realize that all of the musicians were black.

"They're from America," Chaz spoke over the music.

"The entire band?" Usually one or two American jazz players would be accompanied by English musicians. To see an entire band from America was a treat. Just wait until I told Aunt Butty! She'd be gutted to have missed it. Aunt Butty was enamored of all things American.

"Indeed. Here for a couple weeks before they head off to Paris. Very in demand. Aren't they spiffing?"

"Spiffing," I agreed, as the Balboa finished, and the sounds of W. C. Handy's *St. Louis Blues* spilled out into the club. I had a record of Louis Armstrong playing it while Bessie Smith sang. He was better, of course, but this band was astonishingly good.

My gaze was snagged by the pianist. Although dressed identically to the rest of the band, there was something about him—an energy that was almost palpable—that made him stand out from the rest like a tiger amongst house cats.

It was hard to tell how tall he was, but I was guessing tall. His shoulders were broad and straight, filling out his suit rather nicely. His skin was a rich, deep brown, and his dark hair, cut close to a rather nicely shaped skull, was pomaded within an inch of its life, revealing only the tiniest bit of curl.

Maybe it was the heat in his gaze or the slight lift of his full lips as he caught me staring, but there was something about him that sent a shiver right to my toes. A flush rose to my cheeks and I resisted the urge to fan myself. I hadn't blushed like this since I was sixteen.

Fortunately, the waiter arrived at that moment with a highball for me and a sidecar for Chaz. I was tempted to down it in one; instead I sipped it like a proper lady while ordering a second drink.

Chaz raised a brow as the waiter sauntered off. "Plan to get sloshed?"

"If at all possible," I said tartly. Maybe if I drank enough, I'd forget the look that had passed between me and the piano player. It simply wasn't appropriate. Not that appropriateness had ever stopped me from doing exactly as I pleased. Within reason, of course. But I'd a feeling there was nothing at all reasonable going on.

"Care to dance?" Chaz asked languidly.

"But of course." I held out my hand at a delicate angle, the diamond bracelet on my left wrist flashing beneath the chandeliers. He took my hand and pulled me out onto the dancefloor.

The band switched to something slower and altogether sexier. Chaz was a divine dancer. Naturally graceful and athletic with no care as to what others thought. I, on the other hand, was a passing dancer, able to keep up, but only just. There was a great deal of twirling and I found myself quickly becoming breathless. The entire time, the pianist's hot gaze scorched me. It was wildly inappropriate, and yet I couldn't deny the forbidden thrill. What would Felix have said?

Strangely, he'd have likely cheered me on. An oddity for his time, Lord R had never been one to follow society's rules. He refused to let the gossips dictate who he spent time with or called friend. As such, our home had played host to a hodge-podge of peculiar characters during our short marriage. From tarot card reading spiritualists to drunken novelists, Felix enjoyed meeting interesting people regardless of their station. Being insanely rich had a tendency to buffer one from the fallout of such behavior.

Growing up in a vicarage, you'd think I'd have been taught that all men are equal in God's sight. However, it was more a thing preached from the pulpit than practiced in actuality. My father, the vicar of St. Oswin the Good in the tiny Cotswold village of Chipping Poggs, had been something of a crusader for the poor children of Africa. Every Sunday, he would guilt the congregation into donating more than they could afford to his pet cause.

"Even God's poorest creatures are deserving of our charity," he'd say, thumping the pulpit for emphasis. It was literally the most riled papa ever got. In all other aspects of life, he was quite laid back and rather fond of a pint of this or a tipple of that. He spent more time in the pub than he ever did writing a sermon.

And then an Indian man named Mr. Patel moved to the village along with his wife and two children. The children were adorable. Mr. Patel was a gentle and kind man from what I could recall. I mostly remembered his wife's brightly colored silk outfits which shimmered under the watery Cotswold sun. I found them exciting and interesting and wanted to know everything about them and about India. I was certain my dear papa, so enamored of poor African children, would be delighted to meet the Patels and welcome them to our village. For were they not also God's children?

Instead, papa led the charge to run the Patels out of town. "We don't need *their* sort here. Confounded Hinduists!" As if their religion truly had anything to do with it.

Turning to mama for help had been no good. "Your father knows what's best, dear," she'd said, patting my hand before returning to her knitting.

That was all she would say on the matter. Eventually the Patels left, and everyone in Chipping Poggs went back to pretending the distasteful incident had never occurred. Except for me. It had left a bad taste in my mouth and an anger burning in my gut. The minute Aunt Butty offered me a place to stay in London, I jumped at the chance. And that was that. I never returned to Chipping Poggs. Nor did I intend to.

"His name is Hale, by the by. Hale Davis." Chaz's voice jarred me from my memories.

I blinked. "Who is?"

"The pianist you're making googly eyes at." Chaz's lips twitched in amusement. I made an annoyed sound and ignored his inference. Cheeky sod.

Chaz's smile widened. "What about Lord Peter?"

"What about him?"

Lord Peter Varant was about as posh as they come. A peer of the realm and all that. And he'd dabbled at being my suitor for some time now. Oh, he'd never crossed the line—I was in mourning, after all—but he'd made his interest clear in a gentlemanly fashion. Now that the year was up, I expected him to declare himself at any moment. I wasn't entirely sure how I felt about that. Especially since I didn't know what that would mean for Chaz and me. I was fairly certain Lord Varant was aware of the truth about Chaz, but that didn't mean he would approve of his wife running around with another man, and I wasn't going to give up my friendship with Chaz for anyone.

Not to mention I wasn't entirely sure I wanted to be married again. I rather enjoyed my freedom.

"I thought you two had an understanding," Chaz said meaningfully.

I frowned. "Whatever are you going on about?"

"Seems you've caught someone's eye." His own gaze strayed toward the stage.

I fought down a fiery blush. Society matrons—good gosh, was I a matron? —did not blush. "I can't help if a man looks, can I?"

"No. But you can help if you look back." He lifted one eyebrow.

I shot him a dirty look and refused to answer. He wasn't wrong. I was looking. There was a lot to look at and it was very pleasant.

"Doesn't Lord Peter have first dibs?"

"I'm not a race horse. Beside which, I'm not entirely sure I will ever marry again." And Lord Peter was definitely the sort of man who'd insist on marriage.

"Really? You plan on being a nun the rest of your life?" Chaz guffawed at that.

"Heavens, no. Perish the thought. But this *is* 1932. Not the dark ages. Women can vote now and everything."

He whirled me around to get a good look at the pianist again. "And you plan to start your liberation with him?" There was no shock or censure in his tone. Simply mild curiosity. Which was exactly what I expected of Chaz. The world might judge us for our uniqueness, but we always accepted each other exactly as we were.

"Oh, I don't imagine it'll come to that." Despite the heat between us, I couldn't imagine the man would risk his livelihood. Not if he was smart. And I wasn't going to put him in harm's way. "But that doesn't mean I can't enjoy the view. He clearly is." If his steamy gaze was anything to go by.

It occurred to me that the man might be a lady-killer with a woman in every port. For all he knew, Chaz was my husband, and yet here he was making eyes at me across an increasingly crowded dance floor.

The song came to an end, and I dragged Chaz back to the table. I felt flushed and bothered and was in desperate need of another drink. Fortunately, the wait staff was well trained, and I had another highball in my hand before I'd had half a chance to sit down.

"Chaz, darling. How lovely to see you again." The woman who appeared beside our table was tall, willow thin, with golden brown hair that fell in elegant waves to her shoulders. Her face had been done up in "Gardenia," that shockingly pale, waxen look that was so the rage. Her lips were a Chinese red that matched her lacquered nails, and her eyelids were painted a blue which shimmered in the dim light. Her satin evening gown was flesh-colored with a daring V-neckline that very nearly displayed her assets, were she not so nearly flat chested. A multitude of pearl bracelets encircled her left wrist, but she wore no other jewelry.

"Helena!" Chaz rose from his seat and bowed over her hand. "How lovely to see you. Have you met my friend, Lady Rample? Ophelia, this is Helena Fairfax. She *owns* the Astoria Club."

Helena's eyes widened a fraction. "We've never met, but I've heard of you, of course, Lady Rample. Lovely to make your acquaintance."

"Likewise." I'd heard of Helena Fairfax, of course. Who hadn't? Born an Earl's daughter, she'd married beneath her. A mere mister. Well, technically he was the second son of a mere viscount, but as his brother had sired enough brats to start a cricket team, it was unlikely Mr. Fairfax would ever inherit. What was shocking was that Chaz said *she* owned the club. Not her husband. A woman owning a club of any kind was almost unheard of, never mind a jazz club. A woman who was the daughter of a peer was astonishing, to put it mildly.

After assuring herself that we were well taken care of, Helena sauntered off. I might have gawked at her a bit before turning back to Chaz.

"*She* owns the club?" I felt equal parts admiration and glee at the scandal. "How is that possible?"

Chaz gave me a languid smile as he rolled a cigarette. "It's complicated and top secret."

I gave him a look. "Spill."

"Helena has always been an individual. Like you, she's determined not to allow the mores of society to dictate her behavior. Nor will she allow herself to rely on a man. At least, not entirely."

"What does that mean?"

He shrugged and took a sip of his cocktail. "It's well known that Fairfax has little money and is an inveterate gambler. When Helena married him, she was afraid he'd gamble away the money she'd inherited from her mother. She got none from her father, you can imagine. In any case, she invested in this club. Hard to lose money in a place like this. Now she holds the purse strings. Best for all."

"But you said, 'not entirely.' So, she owns the club with someone else."

"Very astute." He nodded toward a dark table in the corner as he blew out an elegant curl of smoke. "Alfred Musgrave. Part owner of the club and front-man. Made his money through... less than savory means. But he's smart and determined to make this place even more successful than it already is. Hence the band all the way from America." His gaze drifted back to the sexy pianist. "I must say, I admire his taste."

I tried exceedingly hard not to look, but it was a useless endeavor. Those dark eyes and that cheeky smile drew me back. I imagined those nimble, dark fingers running over my skin. I was suddenly hot and flustered, an emotion I rarely experience.

I cleared my throat. "Yes. Very talented."

Chaz gave me a knowing look. Which I pointedly ignored. Instead I downed my drink. Chaz held out his hand. "Come, my darling. Let us dance the night away."

"Sounds fabulous, but I need to check my lipstick first."

I found the water closet tucked in the back next to the performers' dressing rooms. After attending to business, I exited the claustrophobic closet only to take the wrong turn down the warren of back halls. I had just discovered my mistake and started to turn around when I heard voices from one of the rooms nearby.

"I'm telling you, I don't like it." The male voice was obnoxiously strident with a nasal twang that was rather common.

"I can't help it if you don't like it, Mr. Musgrave, but I assure you the books are in perfect order." The second voice was female, cultured, very upper crust. It had to be Helena Fairfax.

"Then you won't mind an audit, "Alfred Musgrave bellowed. I picture his unpleasant face twisted in anger with those beady little eyes snapping beneath beetling brows.

"Of course not. Whenever you like. Perhaps tomorrow evening?"

"Very well. We'll meet during the first set."

How interesting. Chaz had said the club was doing well, but Musgrave wanted an audit. Did that mean things weren't going all that well?

I turned to leave and noticed I wasn't the only person eavesdropping. A reedy little man with mousy hair and a prominent Adam's apple hovered near the doorway. His protuberant eyes bulged with fear and his long fingers worried a handkerchief to near threads. The minute he saw me he darted away, as if he didn't want anyone to know he was there.

I wondered vaguely who he was. An admirer of Helena's, perhaps? Likely not. His suit was cheap and his shoes old and scuffed. Not her style. Maybe he worked for the club. A bookkeeper or some such.

With a mental shrug, I made my way back to Chaz. I had reached the opening, ready to step through, when I barreled into a broad chest.

"Whoa, there, little lady." The voice was intrinsically masculine. The hands that grabbed my shoulders to steady me spoke of strength. I glanced up to find myself staring straight into the face of the pianist. Good gosh, why was it so hot all of a sudden? "You all right?"

Was I? "Quite. Thank you," I said in my most British Upper Crust. I stepped carefully away and strode through to the dance floor, my thoughts of the conversation I'd just overheard completed erased by my brush with the pianist.

For the rest of the evening I pretended the pianist was of no interest whatsoever. I'm not entirely sure Chaz believed me.

It was nearly sunrise by the time we staggered up the stairs, bursting into the gray dawn, buzzed on exhaustion and alcohol. The drizzle had stopped, but the air held a distinct chill.

"So, what'd you think, old bean?" Chaz asked, wrapping an arm around my shoulder as we strolled toward the car.

"Brill!" Happiness fizzed inside me. "Jolly good fun. We should come again."

"Wotcha? That you, Chaz?" The words were slurred as the man staggered out of the alleyway running between the Astoria Club and the café next door.

Chaz frowned, stepping slightly in front of me. "Leo. That you? You should be at home." His tone was firm.

The man—Leo—was dressed in stylish evening wear. Not as expensive as Chaz's, but definitely bespoke. His eyes were red rimmed, and he staggered slightly as if drunk. Beads of sweat decorated his upper lip.

"I'm fine." He waved Chaz off and leaned heavily against the brick wall. "Jus' here to meet my wife." He cackled as if he'd told a joke. Frankly, I didn't find the situation amusing in the least.

"Let me help you home, Leo," Chaz insisted, ever the gentleman.

Leo said something extraordinarily rude. Without another word, Chaz marched me toward the car.

"Who was that?" I asked.

"That was Helena's husband, Leo Fairfax."

"Whatever is wrong with him?"

Chaz's expression was pinched. "I don't want to talk about it."

Which only made me more curious. And suspicious. I grabbed his arm. "Come, Chaz. We've been friends far too long for you to pull that sort of nonsense."

He paused next to the car with a heavy sigh. "We used to…run in the same circles."

I frowned, thinking it over. Being familiar with Chaz's preferences and past, there could be more than one. "Which circles specifically?"

"Ones that involved certain substances."

"Oh." What more was there to say?

"Yes, just so."

"Why would you bring me here if you knew Leo's wife owned the club?" Why didn't he stay far away? Why would he put himself in the way of temptation?

"Because I can't let the past control my life, now, can I?"

A stab of guilt hit me. After all, it had been me who'd first administered laudanum to an injured boy. How could I know that the next time we would see each other—a good eight years later—he'd be a disaster, addicted to opium, in debt to his dealer, and afraid his wealthy father would find out? That it would be me— with assistance from my Aunt Butty—who would help him through it all. And now his demons reared their ugly heads again.

"Don't." He gripped my shoulders. "It isn't your fault, Ophelia. None if it was. You were the one who saved me." His eyes were soft.

I swallowed the lump in my throat. I struggled for something meaningful to say and came up with, "Why don't we go to my place for a cup of tea?"

"Not tonight. I'll be fine, old thing. No worries here. Right as rain."

I cast a glance back at Leo's huddled form, barely discernible in the shadows. I reminded myself that Chaz had come a long way in the last eight years, but his words felt forced and worry nested inside me, burrowing its way to my stomach.

With a bright smile, albeit a bit forced, I rejoined Chaz, determined to bury the ghosts of the past and end this evening on a high note. "Come on, darling," I shouted as we clambered into the car, "let's have a jolly tune."

Chaz beamed. "Don't mind if I do, old bean."

We sang *Mad About the Boy* loudly and off-key all the way home. By the time we reached my doorstep, I really believed everything would be aces.

Chapter 3

Light stabbed at my eyes. Who the blue blazes was playing kettle drums inside my skull? I pulled the duvet over my head with a groan.

"Maddie, what are you doing at this ungodly hour?" My voice was muffled by a pile of pillows.

"Sorry, m'lady." Maddie's young voice squeaked alarmingly. "Only it's gone ten and her ladyship says I ought to wake up your ladyship." She sounded as confused as I was.

I risked exposing an eyeball to the blinding light of day. Sure enough, hot pokers stabbed my brain. Why did I let Chaz foist that last highball on me? Oh, right. I'd needed something to cool me down after watching that sexy pianist all night. By gosh, that man could tickle some ivories. I repressed a shiver of delight.

And then I remembered the Leo incident. I hoped Chaz was alright. I really should ring him. Only later. Much later. If I called at this hour, he'd have me drawn and quartered.

Then what Maddie had said penetrated my fogged brain. "What ladyship, Maddie?"

"Her ladyship wot is your aunt, m'lady. She was most insistent." Maggie's tone conveyed just exactly what she thought about *that*.

My aunt. Oh, yes. Aunt Butty. The aunt upon whom I could place the blame of my entire existence. Well, perhaps not entire. I'm certain my parents had something to do with it at some point. But it was Aunt Butty who rescued me from the tedium of the vicarage and whisked me off to the bright lights of London and, eventually, the arms of Lord Rample.

"You did bring tea?" Dear God, I hoped so.

"Yes, m'lady. And also, a glass of water and some headache powders. They're on the nightstand."

How efficient. "God bless you, Maddie."

"As you say, m'lady."

Cheeky minx. I managed to struggle into a sitting position so I could down the foul headache powders followed by an entire pot of Assam tea, liberally sweetened. Meanwhile, Maddie dug around in my wardrobe as though searching for buried treasure, her bony backside stuck up in the air. As a lady's maid, she was an odd one, her accent was pure London, but there was something about her way. Something vaguely…foreign. She was small and dark with shrewd eyes, despite being easily flustered. Still, she made an excellent cup of tea and did wonders for my hair. I could hardly complain.

"What are you looking for?" I asked her.

"The green afternoon dress, m'lady." Her voice was muffled by swath of fabrics. "The one wot her ladyship gave you."

Damnation. Yes. Aunt Butty had gifted me a ghastly olive-green number recently. It did not at all go with my skin tone, which was ivory with pink undertones—very "English rose." Instead it made me look jaundiced. It was, however, one of Aunt Butty's favorite colors. Apparently, that made it a fitting gift for her favorite niece. Although, technically, I was her only niece. I say technically because my mother's brother, my uncle Gerry, is rumored to have more than one family tucked away in the wilds of the English countryside. Bit of a philanderer, that one.

"Good choice, Maddie. For this occasion, anyway. By the by, did my aunt *say* what occasion this was?" Aunt Butty was generally no more a morning person than was I. Arriving at one's abode anywhere near ten of the clock was unheard of. In fact, she rarely arose before noon. Sad when one's aunt has more of a social life, but then I had an excellent excuse. Or rather, I *had* an excellent excuse. I really needed to get a life. An evening with Chaz was an excellent start.

"No, m'lady." Maddie popped out of the wardrobe with the ghastly gown in hand, thin cheeks flushed so that the faint scar under her right eye stood out. "But she was quite excitable."

That wasn't saying much. Butty's state of being was excitable. So much so that no one commented on it unless the excitement became more pronounced than usual.

"Oh, dear." I downed my cup of tea and stared longingly at the nearly full pot before pushing it away. "I guess we'd better hurry, then."

Maddie helped me into the dress and removed the silk scarf from around my head. The scarf had done its trick and kept my golden brown, shoulder-length waves in place, so after a quick sprucing up and smoothing a few flyaways, I was on my way to hear whatever disaster Aunt Butty had gotten herself into. Not that she would claim a disaster. More likely she'd consider it a Grand Adventure.

Like the time she'd fallen from a camel, broken her leg, and ended up the guest of some sheik or other. Most people would consider it an Unfortunate Incident. Aunt Butty considered it an Opportunity. Aunt Butty spin a much better tale than Sir Eustace.

I found my aunt perched on the edge of a blue velvet settee looking for all the world like she was about to take flight. And I don't just mean the fact that she literally had a bird stuck on her head.

"Aunt Butty, darling, whatever are you wearing?" I asked as we exchanged cheek kisses.

She touched a purple feather that dipped dangerously low. "Like it? Marcel's latest creation."

"It... makes a statement."

The wide, straw concoction was more suited to the reign of the late King Edward than to 1932. Someone had divested a bird of its feathers, dyed them puce, and rammed them back into a vague semblance of an exotic fowl, complete with curled ostrich feathers in a violent shade of lime. It was beyond hideous and clashed with my aunt's ultra-modern, belted crepe de chine in eye-searing yellow. On the other hand, some clever minx had managed to design the garment so that its slim lines somehow suited Aunt Butty's plump waistline and ample bosom. I was going to have to bribe her for the name of her dressmaker. My own figure was far more similar to my aunt's than fashion currently dictated. A fact that Lady Chatelain and her ilk were quick to point out. I was just as quick to remind them that I, at least, had a personality more interesting than wet paste.

I slouched onto the slipper chair opposite my aunt, hoping she'd notice my dress. She didn't. Nor did she glare at me for slouching. Something was most assuredly up.

Abandoning my slouch, I poured tea, dropping in the three lumps of sugar she preferred. Aunt Butty had always been there for me. The least I could do was listen to whatever silliness she'd been up to.

"What's wrong, Auntie?" I asked, handing her a teacup hand-painted with adorable little blue flowers.

"What makes you think something is wrong?" She took the cup and sipped delicately, giving a smile of satisfaction. Maddie really did make an excellent pot of tea.

"You're in my townhouse before noon," I said dryly.

"Oh, that." She waved airily. "I am, perhaps, a tad overstimulated, but nothing is *wrong*, per se."

Butty was a bit... eccentric. As were many of the wealthy Upper Crust. In her younger years, she'd been something of a Bohemian. The tales she used to tell of her sojourns in Paris... delightful. Wicked.

"Do tell," I murmured around my own cup. With the induction of a second dose of tea, I was starting to feel almost human.

She carefully selected a biscuit and eyed it before announcing, "I've had intimate relations with a man."

I nearly spat my tea. "Well..." I had nowhere to go. Butty's lovers were numerous. Or they had been. She'd slowed somewhat in her advancing years—her words, not mine. She was only twenty years older than my own thirty-five. "I'm certain that's... true."

She lifted a beringed hand, soft and powdered, to tuck a lock of graying hair behind her ear. The scent of roses always clung to her. I could never pass by the flowers without being reminded of my aunt. "It's not what you think, dear. He's..." She leaned forward as if parting a dreadful secret. "*American.*"

I nearly burst out laughing. Until I remembered the smoldering, midnight gaze of Hale Davis, the jazz pianist. He was American. Surely not...

"Where, ah, did you meet this... American?"

She settled back into the settee and took a delicate sip of her tea followed by a nibble of cream biscuit. "I met him at Bertram's."

Couldn't have anything to do with the jazz people, then. Bertram's was very posh, very upscale, very expensive. Pheasants under glass. That sort of thing. Definitely not the sort of place for jazz. Or musicians. They'd likely turn up their noses at Beethoven himself.

"I was with Louise."

"Well, that explains it."

She gave me an arch look. "And what exactly is that supposed to mean?"

"Louise Pennyfather gets you into more trouble than anyone I know." As if Aunt Butty needed help. She and her bosom friend were a constant breath away from scandal. And they reveled in it. I supposed that at the advanced age of fifty-something, they had a right to it.

Butty snorted. "Be that as it may, she introduced me to this gorgeous man. Friend of her husband's. Horace Bronson. From some place called Texas. It's in America."

"I'm familiar. Cowboy?"

"Hardly. More like cow owner." She frowned. "What do they call them?"

"Rancher, I believe." I practically saw dollar signs dancing in Butty's eyes. "Sounds... intriguing."

"Indeed."

"What's the problem then?" I asked.

She sighed heavily and downed the rest of her tea. "He's married."

"Since when has that ever stopped you?" Aunty Butty had been married thrice. Each husband had died leaving her richer than ever. And not a one of them had ever suspected she had a tendency to dally with whatever handsome gent roamed too close, up to and including the

Irish gardener. Not that I blamed her. The man had been wickedly handsome and those blue eyes...

Besides, none of her husbands had been particularly faithful. The most recent one had cast off this mortal coil in the bed of a chorus girl.

"I have made it my personal rule to never get involved with *happily* married men," Butty announced piously.

"He couldn't have been too happily married if he hopped into bed with you." And it wasn't like she needed his money or his hand in marriage. Aunt Butty was nearly as rich as I was and had sworn off marriage for good.

"True." She mulled it over. "His wife *did* sound awful."

In my experience, married men who wished to cheat always made their wives sound awful. "Well, then, I don't see what the problem is."

She thrust out her wrist dramatically. "He gave me this."

A bauble of gold and diamonds sparkled on her left wrist. I eyed it carefully. "Stunning. Expensive." Certainly a costly gift for a woman one had only just met. Butty had that effect on men. A French count had once given her an entire sarcophagus. I think she still had it at her country estate.

She sighed. "And not my taste in the slightest."

It was true. Aunt Butty much preferred enameled whatsis from the Far East. Lots of color and exotic geometry. "Well, he'll probably go back to Texas soon enough and you can be rid of the thing." It was a bit ostentatious.

She stared at it a moment longer. "I would have preferred a Bentley."

"You can't drive," I reminded her. I was usually the one who had to chauffeur her about in my own Mercedes Roadster. I didn't mind. I loved to drive.

"Regardless, it would have been much more fun. Although, I must say, what I did to get it was *vastly* fun. These Texas men have such large—."

"More tea, Auntie?" I interrupted. Lord knows I did not need a detailed run down of my aunt's sexual exploits.

"What did *you* get up to last night, dear?" she asked, holding out her cup.

I told her about Sir Eustace's boring party and how Chaz had rescued me. "My first time at a jazz club. It was..." The pianist popped into my mind. "It was an adventure," I finished lamely.

"Your father would not approve." She said it with glee rather than censure. She was right. The vicar would not at all approve. In fact, he'd be scandalized. The thought gave me almost as much glee as it did my aunt. "Is that the place Helena Fairfax runs?"

I lifted a brow, only partially surprised. Aunt Butty seemed to know everything that went on in London. Even some of the seedier aspects. "You know about that?"

She chuckled. "A woman in business? Naturally."

I realized perhaps Aunt Butty could assuage my curiosity about Helena's husband without having to involve Chaz. "Have you met her husband, Leo?"

Aunt Butty made a face. "Nasty man. She could have done better. Although he is rather handsome."

I'd been so wrapped up in his behavior, I hadn't noticed. "Is he… Does he have an opium problem?"

She snorted. "Understatement. I believe he's what they call a dope fiend." No doubt she gotten that from one of those Hollywood films she was so fond of. "The one time I tried opium in Paris, I admit it was rather relaxing, but that was in my younger days. It was all the rage. Everyone was doing it. But I know too many who have lost years and fortunes to the rot. Let's just say I shall never try it again."

"How exotic." I wasn't certain how else to react. I knew opium was popular among a certain type of person, but that wasn't the crowd I chose to surround myself with. And fortunately, now, neither did Chaz. "After what Chaz went through, I've no intention of trying it."

"Which is very intelligent of you. It's terrible stuff, as you well know. Word is, Leo's got some Chinese connection or other. He's spent half the last decade addicted to the stuff. Such a shame. Why do you ask?"

I told her about our run-in with Leo the previous evening. "Chaz was… displeased."

"Well, that's because he is a gentleman. The boy has very delicate sensibilities." Aunt Butty was one of the few people who knew the truth about Chaz. "Not to mention, well, you know about his past. Poor thing. Hope this doesn't upset him too much."

"I think I boosted his spirits enough by the end of the night. And I'll be sure and check in on him." Just in case.

Our conversation turned back to the evening at the club. I thought about mentioning the pianist, but I didn't. That was my little secret. Instead I described the décor, the music, and who among the upper echelons of society had been in attendance.

Aunt Butty sighed. "It reminds me of this one time in Cairo. I met the most divine man at a nightclub. That man could kiss! You would never believe the things he could do with his—."

Just then Maddie barreled through the door. Alas, I was never to know what Butty's man in Cairo could do.

"This came fer y'r ladyship." Maddie slapped a stack of envelopes in my hand and marched out. I had no idea if she was in a huff because she found our conversation shocking, or if she was simply being herself. One never knew with Maddie.

Aunt Butty stared after her askance. "You know, you really could afford better help."

"Of course, I could. But they wouldn't be as interesting, now, would they, darling?" I gave her a sly smile. "Besides, your Flora isn't exactly the best trained maid I've ever seen."

She shook her head, ignoring my jab. "Well, I must be off. By the by, I'm having a small dinner party tonight. Be there."

I sighed. "Truly, Aunt, would it have hurt you to give a bit more notice? What if I were attending a party this evening?"

"Pish posh," she said airily as she wrapped herself in her fox stole. The orange hue clashed hideously with the rest of her outfit. "Be there. Lord Varant will be." She had the audacity to wink on her way out the door.

Chapter 4

After Butty took her leave, I eyeballed the stack of post Maddie had so unceremoniously dumped on me. No doubt invitations to more tedious soirees where another Sir Somebody would drone on about his so-called adventures. I dumped the lot onto a pile of other, similar envelopes which still needed opened. I had no intention of doing so any time soon.

So, Lord Varant would be at Butty's soiree. I was oddly nervous about facing him. We hadn't seen each other in some time and I both wanted to make an impression and equally wanted him to know I didn't care what he thought. What to wear? Something devastating, that was for sure.

I paced the sitting room, restlessness stirring my soul. That strange agitation that is half boredom and half something else. I couldn't sit still, and yet I didn't want to *do* anything, either. And there were several hours yet until Aunt Butty's dinner party. I needed to get out of the house.

I dashed upstairs and quickly divested myself of the green tragedy. I didn't bother calling Maddie. No doubt she was nipping the sherry by now. I decided upon a pair of black, wide legged trousers paired with a cherry red, short sleeved jumper and matching pumps. Feeling quite chic in a new trench, I yelled down into the kitchen that I was leaving and hustled out to my Mercedes parked at the curb, its top up in deference to the drizzly weather.

Although Felix had left me a stable full of cars, the Mercedes 710 SSK Roadster was far and away my favorite. It was a delicious cobalt blue with a top speed of 120 miles per hour! The fastest car of its day. Alas, I could rarely crank it up to top speed as London roads were a bit tight for that, but on my occasional trip out to the country, I'd open her up and let her go.

Lord R had been a strong proponent of women driving, much to the horror of his peers. He claimed to all and sundry that liberated womanhood could only be for the good of all. And, fortunately for me, that meant a stunner of a cobalt motor all to myself. Not much of a driver himself, Felix had his chauffeur teach me to drive. The man used to be a test driver for a motorcar company. Perhaps that's where I picked up my love of driving fast.

Heads turned as I gunned the engine and took off in a screech of tires. I admit, I enjoyed the attention a little too much as I zipped through the streets of London past white-washed Georgian townhouses and looming Victorian facades. Driving was a favorite pastime, but still it didn't distract me from memories of bedroom eyes staring at me from over a piano. Maybe I could use my powers of persuasion and convince Chaz to revisit the jazz club tonight.

I'd parked the car and was headed toward Harrod's and a new dress when a woman nearly plowed into me. We both stumbled to a stop.

"So sorry," she mumbled, hardly looking at me.

I recognized her immediately. "Helena Fairfax?"

She blinked, big eyes rimmed in thick kohl were a little glassy. Did she have a drug problem, too? Or was she merely distracted?

"Yes? Sorry, have we met?" Her butter-yellow handbag matched her shoes and she clutched it a little tighter. I wondered vaguely if I should be offended.

"Last night at your..." I hesitated. Her ownership of the Astoria Club was a secret. "I'm friends with Chaz Raynott. We met last night. At the Astoria."

Her brow unfurrowed and something like relief crept into her gaze. "Oh, yes, I remember." She touched the tips of her fingers to her forehead. "Sorry. I'm... a little distracted."

"No worries. You look like you could use a good cup of tea."

"You've no idea." Her laugh was like tinkling glass, bright but a little brittle. It matched her glassy gaze.

"Why don't you join me, then? Let's go to Brown's. We can take my car." I wasn't sure why I asked, other than that I was a nosy git. Besides, tea and cakes were always a grand idea.

She hesitated. "Why not?"

"Fabulous!"

Back in the car we climbed, Helena looking a tiny bit nervous. "You know how to drive?"

"Naturally, darling. Hold on to your hat!" I swung into traffic and gunned it, swerving around cars and pedestrians. Horns tooted in my wake. Helena literally held on to her hat, face pale, lips pressed firmly together. Her eyes lost some of their glassiness. I don't think she breathed until I pulled the car up to the curb and turned off the engine.

The wood-paneled tea room at Brown's Hotel was doing a brisk business. In the far corner stood a grand piano gleaming beneath crystal chandeliers. From it elicited the sounds of a classical tune. Something mellow. Chopin, perhaps. A white-jacketed waiter with an impressive red moustache led us to a square table draped in an equally white linen cloth set with two places in silver and bone china.

"Tea, My Lady? Madam?" He bowed to me and then to Helena. I gave him points for knowing how to address us properly. I wondered if the headwaiter had whispered our identities in his ear.

"Assam for me."

"Darjeeling," Helena said.

More wait staff arrived with steaming pots of tea and tiered trays loaded with an assortment of delectable delights. Helena took a cucumber sandwich without looking, but I eyed every morsel carefully. As well as cucumber, there was egg and cress, smoked salmon, and roast beef. The second tier held half a dozen plain scones—pots of clotted cream and strawberry jam made their appearance along with lumps of sugar and a jar of cream for the tea. The top tier was overflowing with tea cakes, Seville orange tea biscuits, frosted ginger cake, and an assortment of other goodies. I selected a few items for my plate.

"I was astonished to discover that you own the, ah, venue," I said as I poured tea. I didn't want to embarrass her by blabbing about her connections. After all, it just wasn't done for women of our class.

She smiled tightly, gaze sliding to the other patrons as she squeezed lemon into her tea. No one paid us any mind. "Oh?" Her tone was entirely non-committal.

"I think it's wonderful," I continued, taking a bite of egg and cress. Truly scrumptious. The perfect amount of mayonnaise-to-egg ratio. Dabbing delicately at the corner of my mouth I said, "A true sign of independence and equality. You should be proud."

She visibly relaxed, finally nibbling on the cucumber finger. "Not everyone thinks so."

"Some people are idiots," I said firmly. "I'm so curious as to how you came to be a business woman. I've often considered it myself." Until that moment, I'd done no such thing, but Helena Fairfax needn't know that. I bit into a ginger cake. Delightful! Spicy and sweet and so very moist. It melted in my mouth like mana from Heaven!

She shrugged slightly as she sipped her tea. "There wasn't much choice. I'm sure if you know Chaz he has explained my... situation."

"Yes. Rather. Men." I gave an exasperated sigh. Not everyone was so lucky in marriage as I had been. Although Lord R and I may not have had a Grand Passion, we did have friendship and kindness—which stands for a lot, if you ask me. Not to mention, he left me a great deal of money. "Although—and I know this is terribly nosy—I do find your choice of partner... curious." Alfred Musgrave was decidedly of the lower classes. No two ways about that. Far too rough for a woman like Helena or a place like the Astoria Club, which clearly catered to the upper crust.

She took another fortifying sip of tea. "It wasn't my choice," she admitted. Leaning forward she said, "You promise this goes no further?"

I was surprised she would confide in me at all. "Of course."

"My husband got into debt with this Musgrave person. I would have let Leo deal with it on his own, but Musgrave threatened my club. I had no choice but to bring him in as partner." Her features were tight. Angry. I couldn't say as I blamed her. "He is not the sort of person I enjoy associating with. Much too crass. However, he is rather brilliant at this business stuff. We've never been busier."

"Indeed." I wanted to ask more, particularly after overhearing the conversation of the previous night, but the stiffness of her spine and the tightness of her expression told me it was pointless. She was done talking about her business partner. I switched to a lighthearted tone as I plucked a Seville orange tea biscuit from the tiered tray. "By the way, the band you brought in from America? Divine, darling. So talented. I've never heard anything like them."

"Oh, yes." She took out a slim, ivory cigarette holder, fit a cigarette to the end, and lit it before drawing in a deep lungful of smoke. "That was Alfred's idea. Spiffing, aren't they?" She blew smoke rings at the ceiling from between carnelian lips. Very chic. Very elegant. "Wait until you hear the singer they brought with them. Coco Starr. She had a touch of laryngitis last night, but she'll be on tonight and tomorrow."

"I look forward to hearing her."

"You'll be there, then?" She feigned disinterest, but there was an eagerness to her which was dashed odd.

"I have a dinner party tonight, but Chaz promised to take me dancing again, so perhaps after." Chaz had promised no such thing, but I'd no doubt I could convince him without much effort. I pretended my eagerness had everything to do with music and nothing to do with Hale Davis. Dare I ask Helena about him? Probably not. I wouldn't want her getting the wrong idea. Not that I was sure what the right idea was...

With no clue how to prolong the conversation, we fell into awkward silence, sipping our tea and poking at tiny cakes. Well, Helena poked. Frankly, I'm not one to waste perfectly good cake, regardless of size. Which is, no doubt, why my hips were slightly wider than fashion currently dictated.

We talked about the weather and mutual acquaintances in that vague way English people do when they're being polite to someone they barely know. Finally, before it got too painful, Helena begged leave and I cheerfully assured her I had my own errands to run. If I was going to drag Chaz to the Astoria Club, the occasion called for a new gown.

"Can I give you a lift anywhere?" I asked.

"No, thank you. My husband is picking me up." She gave me a tight smile.

There went any hope of pumping her for more information. "Well, then, I hope to see you tonight."

We bid our goodbyes and I started down the pavement toward my Mercedes until I decided a bit of a stroll would do me good. Helena was still standing curb side, waiting for her husband. I was halfway up the block toward her, when a big, black Rolls motored up to the curb. Only it wasn't Helena's husband who stepped out. It was Alfred Musgrave.

How peculiar. Helena clearly didn't like the man, so why was she getting a lift from him? And why had she told me her husband was picking her up? My suspicion was immediately aroused. I just wasn't sure what to be suspicious about. With another man I might have thought affair, but Musgrave was decidedly unlikeable, and it was clear Helena felt the same.

Musgrave assisted Helena into the motor, then popped around to the driver's side. Just as he opened the door, a Morris Minor Saloon came barreling out of nowhere. It swung around the corner, wobbled wildly, and veered toward Musgrave's Rolls, out of control. I only had enough time to notice the driver's rather unusual tweed fedora pulled low over his face before Musgrave let out a shout. It was too late; the other car hit him, knocking him over. It didn't even slow as it screeched down the road and around the next corner, disappearing from sight.

For half a tick I stood there, frozen. And then Helena started screaming.

Shéa MacLeod

Chapter 5

I took off down the pavement at a fast trot, the only speed my pumps would allow. Ignoring Helena, I rounded the Rolls to find Musgrave flat on his back, a trickle of blood seeping from his forehead. Good gosh! He'd been killed!

Then Musgrave stirred and moaned, jarring me from my overactive imaginings. I clattered to his side and helped him to his feet. He was a sturdy fellow, so it wasn't easy. "Are you all right?" I blathered, possibly somewhat in shock. I'd never seen a person mowed down before, though with the way people drove around London, it was a surprise it didn't happen more often. I glanced around for help, but other than Helena, the street was nearly empty. The doorman was nowhere to be seen. "We should call the police. That nitwit nearly killed you." My heart rate was still somewhere in the rafters, but my training had begun to kick in. Once a war nurse, always a war nurse, I suppose. I reminded myself I'd seen much worse than a man toppled by a car during the Great War.

"No police," he said firmly as I guided him to the pavement. He fished a cheap cotton handkerchief from his pocket and pressed it to his bleeding forehead. "I'm fine. A bit battered. Nothing to worry about."

"Are you sure, Mr. Musgrave?" I asked. "It looked dreadful."

By now, the doorman had returned to his station and was trying to calm Helena to no avail. Two women walked by, trying not to stare, but failing miserably.

"Just an accident." Musgrave patted my hand. His was a bit sweaty and reeked of musk and hair oil. "No need to worry, my dear. Helena, would you stop that infernal screeching?"

Helena's screams turned to hiccupping whimpers. It surprised me that such a stalwart businesswoman would fall to pieces over the misfortunes of a loathsome business partner. But what did I know? We all have our weaknesses, I suppose.

"If you're sure," I said, untangling my arm from Musgrave's and stepping back. "But I do think you should see a doctor. And she," I nodded to Helena, "should probably take something for the shock." Like a good shot of whiskey. Which didn't sound bad, come to think of it.

"Kind of you, my dear, but don't worry your pretty head." That last was said with a sly and rather lascivious wink.

I grimaced, suddenly feeling less charitable and a lot more sympathetic toward the driver who'd nearly missed him. "If you're sure."

"I will be fine," he assured me.

I wasn't so sure, but he clambered into the car and motored off, Helena still looking shell-shocked beside him. With a mental shake of the head, I went about my business, trying to forget the image of the car plowing over Musgrave. And that dashed odd hat. A fedora in some ghastly tweed of green and yellow. Wouldn't soon be forgetting that monstrosity.

It took two flutes of champagne at the dressmaker's, but I managed a semblance of amnesia, emerging some time later laden with shopping bags and feeling somewhat giddy despite seeing Musgrave almost flattened in front of my eyes. I promised myself it was the joy of shopping, not the copious amounts of alcohol.

The moment I got home I rang up Chaz. Felix had been of the firm belief that all the best homes had telephones, which was why mine was prominently displayed in the hall. Chaz liked his modern toys and had no less than three in his flat. Excessive, but that was Chaz.

"Hello, darling," I chirped as soon as he answered. I wanted to ask how he was, but was suddenly afraid to do so. Instead I said, "Put on your dancing togs and pick me up tonight. I'll be at Aunt Butty's."

"Dash it, Ophelia, I meant to go to my club tonight," he pouted. Like any man of his class, Chaz belonged to a stuffy gentleman's club. The same one, no doubt, as his father and grandfather before him.

"What a yawn, darling. You know you'll have more fun with me. Besides, I've got such juicy gossip for you."

"See you at eleven." He rang off. Chaz never could resist a good chin wag.

Aunt Butty lived in a large flat on the edge of Soho. In truth, she owned the entire building and rented out the other flats to artists, musicians, and writers. Quite shocking for a woman of her status, but Aunt Butty enjoyed the Bohemian life and her flat suited her just fine. She much preferred it to her country house, or the Mayfair townhouse.

I was met at the door by a dusty-skinned butler dressed in a cream-silk sherwani embroidered in gold over matching silk pyjama. On his head, he wore an intricately wrapped dastar in a rich pavo blue and his face was graced with a luxurious black beard. His thick eyebrows made him look rather fierce, but I knew him to be a gentle soul.

"Good evening, My Lady," he intoned in his carefully modulated voice. I'd no idea where my aunt had picked up the Sikh gentleman and convinced him to play butler, but he was a cherished member of her rather unusual household.

"Good evening, Mr. Singh," I said as he took my coat. I'd wanted to wear the purple velvet, but as it was drizzling, I'd settled for the black wool with the rabbit fur collar. "How are you?"

"Very good, My Lady."

Mr. Singh still carried the lilting accent of his homeland, India. He was very mysterious, even to Aunt Butty. None of us knew his first name. He'd simply been "Mr. Singh" since the day he arrived at her house. She claimed to like the look of him and didn't care if he was cagey about his past. Very Aunt Butty behavior. She could be cagey herself.

"Cocktails are being served in the sitting room, My Lady."

"Very good. Thank you, Mr. Singh." I made my way into Aunt Butty's sitting room. On a good day, it tended to be overcrowded with items she'd collected on her travels: Egyptian goddesses, wooden masks from Africa, perfume bottles from Marrakesh. Currently, it was packed with guests in evening togs, trying not to jostle each other's drinks.

A gentleman in a plum velvet smoking jacket sat at Aunt Butty's grand piano tinkling out some absurd and slightly dirty ditty. A woman I recognized as a popular stage actress entertained several men in the corner. Aunt Butty held court from her chaise longue, smiling benevolently at all from beneath a rose-pink turban festooned with diamonds and feathers.

I wanted to ask my aunt about Helena's possible drug use, but now was not the time. Instead, I gave her a little finger wave and looked about me for a drink.

Someone handed me a tumbler filled with amber liquid. "I believe you favor the highball."

For one heart stopping moment, I forgot where I was and simply stared like an idiot. Lord Peter Varant had the enviable position of looking rather like the divine American actor, Gary Cooper. What the man did to a tuxedo should be illegal.

"You remembered. Thank you." I took the drink from him, proud that I managed to get out a full sentence without sounding moronic.

"Of course I remember." His voice was a low rumble. "I remember everything."

I swallowed. "Well, isn't that something." Lord, could I be any more inane?

I'd met Lord Varant shortly after I married Felix. It had been one of those numerous, boring parties we'd seemed forced to attend. Felix had wandered off with some Lord Whatsis or other for cigars and whiskey. I was left to my own devices. Technically, I suppose I was meant to mingle with the other ladies, but being new to this particular social stratum and having no friends among them, I was more or less an outcast. After all, the new Lady Rample was a mere vicar's daughter with no money of her own. I'd yet to find my way among them and so keenly felt my *otherness*.

And so, I'd been feeling rather out of sorts and uncertain of myself until Lord Varant made it his business to keep me entertained and introduced me around at the party. I will never forget his kindness.

While Lord Varant had never been anything but a gentleman, his interest had been clear from the get-go. After Felix died, I'd expected Lord Varant to pursue me, but other than flowers for the funeral and the occasional solicitous note to ensure I was well, he'd made no advances. Aunt Butty had assured me that after the appropriate year of mourning, he'd be on my doorstep. Well, the year was up and he'd yet to arrive. It baffled me no end. Still, it was clear in his manner that he found me as attractive as ever. Men. I swear I shall never understand them if I live to be a hundred.

"I hadn't realized Aunt Butty had invited you to her little soiree."

"She doesn't usually," he admitted. "But we happened to run into each other recently, and she insisted."

"Did she now?" How convenient of her. I gave my aunt a hard stare. She must have felt my gaze for she looked up, grinned wickedly, and gave me a little finger wave.

"How have you been holding up, My Lady?" Lord Varant asked.

"Well enough, thank you. Life goes on." It was the British way. Stiff upper lip and all that.

"I must apologize for not calling sooner. I've been away in the country. Some matters on my estate needed tending to, but I'm back in town for the season and hope to see more of you."

I smiled, pleased by the attention. "I'm certain that can be arranged."

I couldn't help but compare Lord Peter Varant to Hale Davis. Both men were ridiculously handsome, but where Lord Varant was smooth sophistication and quiet smolder, Hale was raw, blatant sexuality. Lord Varant clearly belonged in my world. Hale just as clearly did not. And yet I found them both quite intriguing.

A gong sounded from the hallway.

"Ladies and gentlemen!" Aunt Butty clapped her hands. "Dinner is served. Gentlemen, please escort your assigned lady."

Lord Varant held out his arm gallantly. "My Lady."

"You were assigned to me, were you, My Lord?" Aunt Butty no doubt interfering again.

Lord Varant smiled a bit coyly, I thought, and escorted me into the dining room.

The room, despite being in a mere flat, was large enough to contain a table that seated sixteen. Aunt Butty had her entire Royal Doulton Berkshire set out with its green and gold trim, plus enough crystal to blind a person. Once everyone was seated, Mr. Singh made the rounds with a bottle of wine.

Lord Varant was seated at my left. On my right was a gentleman I'd met only briefly before. He was fiftyish and handsome in a dissipated way, as if he'd spent too much of his youth overindulging in booze and food. He immediately monopolized me.

"My Lady, perhaps you remember. Wilburton Huxton. We met at the Winter Ball held by the Duchess of Kent."

"Ah, yes." I vaguely remembered. It had been shortly before I met and married Felix. If memory served, at the time Huxton had been drunk and completely uninterested in a penniless girl from a small village in the Cotswolds. That he now found me fascinating was unlikely due to the elegance of my evening gown and the rumors of just how much Lord Rample had left in my bank account.

"I was so sorry to hear about your terrible loss." His voice oozed with faux sympathy.

"Thank you." I tried to turn back to Lord Varant, but I suddenly felt a hand on my thigh. Very *high* on my thigh.

In shock, I turned to stare at Huxton. He gave me an oily smile. So, I did what any decent woman would do. I smiled back with cloying sweetness. Then I took my fish fork, slipped it beneath the table, and stabbed the blighter in the hand.

Huxton let out a yelp. The entire table turned to stare at him.

"Is everything all right?" Aunt Butty asked.

Huxton gave her a pained smile. "Oh, yes, quite. I, er, have a sore tooth," he said lamely.

"Oh, dear, do you need to go home? Perhaps Mr. Singh can call the doctor?"

"No, no. Thank you. I shall soldier on."

And soldier on he did, but he didn't say a word to me the rest of the evening.

Chapter 6

The joint was jumping, the wail of the saxophone cutting through the cheerful chatter and blue clouds of cigarette smoke hanging over the Astoria Club. Helena sashayed toward us the moment we walked in, swathed in a slinky gown of shimmering silver. Long, drop earrings hung nearly to her shoulders. At first, I thought they were real rubies, but as she drew closer their shine gave them away. They were very good paste, which struck me as odd.

She thrust a highball glass at me, which I took gratefully. Gone was the tortured woman of earlier. In her place was a cool, calculated dame, worthy of a Marlene Dietrich role. Will the real Helena Fairfax please stand up?

She gave Chaz air kisses before showing us to the same table as before. She gave me a knowing look. "Good view of the band."

I gave her a tight smile. I found this sudden shift in personality confusing. Was she, perhaps, embarrassed at revealing so much emotion earlier? "Divine."

"Josette is about to come on."

"Josette?" Chaz asked, his smooth tenor carrying easily over the noisy club.

"Josette Margaux, our singer," Helena supplied. "Alfred discovered her in France. Charming girl. Very talented." There was something hard and cold in her expression. A tightening around the eyes. "Much better than Coco Starr. *She* came with the band. American. Very brassy."

How odd. She'd rhapsodized over Coco only the previous night. "I look forward to hearing Josette," I said cheerfully, taking a sip of my highball. It was perfect.

"I'll catch you later," she said vaguely, drifting away to greet another couple who'd just entered.

"She's a peculiar one, don't you think?" I asked Chaz.

"All the inbreeding. You know how us upper crust sorts are."

I snickered, being only vaguely related to the upper crust despite my title and ridiculous amount of brass. My people weren't exactly common, but close enough to it. Not that it ever bothered Felix one wit. And I've found that money often talks louder than bloodlines, even among the ton. Especially if you've enough of a bloodline to brag about it.

The music paused, the lights dimmed, and an expectant hush fell over the crowd. Hale Davies tickled the ivories with a little flourish, dark gaze locked on mine. I felt myself flush in the most unladylike places.

Just then, a man stumbled through the front door. He was clearly drunk, staggering between the tables, slapping everyone on the back with forced bonhomie. He was in perhaps his early forties, handsome, but with a weak chin.

"I recognize that man," I said to Chaz. "Who is it?"

"Helena's husband, Leo Fairfax," Chaz muttered. "Quite the winner, eh?"

"Quite," I said dryly. "He's the man we saw outside the club last night, isn't he?"

Chaz shifted uncomfortably. "Yes." His tone was final. In fact, when Leo waved at him, Chaz pointedly turned his back.

Helena also made a point of ignoring her husband, even when he shouted at her across the room. The head waiter arrived and ushered him quickly toward the bar. I was half surprised Helena didn't have bouncers throw him out.

I was about to breathe a sigh of relief when Leo pushed away from the bar and sauntered toward us. "Chaz." His words were as heavily slurred as they had been the previous night. "Old buddy. Long time. We've missed you."

Chaz's face was white, pinched. His fists were clenched. "Get away from me, Leo."

"Come now," Leo taunted. "We're having a party tomorrow. You should come. Plenty for everyone."

Chaz went from white to red. I was afraid he'd punch Leo in the face then and there. Granted, Leo deserved it, but I knew Chaz would hate drawing that sort of attention to himself. So I did the first thing that popped into my head. I leaned over and stomped on Leo's instep with my heel, giving it an extra grind for good measure.

Leo let out a howl of pain and I tittered an apology, playing up the drunken idiot angle. Granted, I was a bit buzzed, but not near so far gone I couldn't control myself.

Helena, the headwaiter at her side, came rushing over. "Is everything all right?"

"Get him away from me, Helena." Chaz's voice, usually so full of charm, was barely more than a snarl simmering with rage.

Helena nodded to the headwaiter, and the man gripped Leo's arm, steering him away. "Come now, sir. I've called a cab for you."

"Don't need no cab," Leo slurred.

"Of course not, sir." The headwaiter managed to manhandle Leo out of the club and up the stairs. I breathed a sigh of relief.

"I'm sorry," Helena said softly. Chaz ignored her, but I gave her a grateful smile.

And then from behind the stage curtains came a wisp of a thing. Hardly more than a girl, really, with shiny black hair cut short and smoothed down. Her skin was a dusky almost golden taupe, shimmering beneath the spotlight as if dusted with diamonds. Her wide eyes were heavily rimmed in kohl, drawn out into points in the Egyptian style. Her full lips were painted carnelian red, mesmerizing.

When she opened those red lips, the sound that spilled out was rich, throaty, magical. I blinked, stunned, as goose flesh rose on my arms. How could such a tiny thing produce such sound? It made me shiver right down to my toes.

"All of me. Why not take all of me? Can't you see, I'm no good without you..." Josette crooned into the microphone. Her long fingers played with the stand, stroking it lightly, suggestively.

Behind her, the band played slow, meaningful, sexy. Almost against my will, my gaze slid toward the pianist. He wasn't looking at me, instead he focused on his hands skimming over the keyboard. I toyed with asking Helena to introduce us, but that might raise her suspicions. Chaz could ask for an introduction without raising eyebrows, but I could imagine the mocking he'd give me if I suggested it.

As the last notes of the song died away, my attention was snagged by a commotion near the door. Alfred Musgrave had arrived looking none the worse for wear after his brush with death other than a sticking plaster on his forehead. A scrawny man hustled up, face pinched as if his shoes hurt. I recognized him as the man who'd overheard Musgrave and Helena's argument. Musgrave pushed him away and barreled past as the band struck up the next song, something zippy and bright as champagne bubbles.

I watched as Musgrave disappeared through a door, half hidden by drapes, next to the bar and vaguely recalled the argument I'd overheard between him and Helena the previous night. Must be in regard to that audit he was talking about. Which reminded me that I should probably schedule an audit with my own business manager at some point in the near future. Not that there was anything amiss, but I liked to stay on top of things. "Never trust anyone with your money," Lord R always told me. "You've got to keep an eye on it yourself." And I planned to. I did not want to have to move in with Aunt Butty, much as I loved her. Nor did I want to run back to Chipping Poggs. Perish the thought.

"Chaz, are you sure the club is doing well?" I asked.

"Seems to be. Why do you ask?"

I cast another glance toward the door through which Musgrave had disappeared. "I overheard Musgrave telling Helena he wanted an audit."

Chaz shrugged. "Don't mean a thing, old bean. Audits happen in business all the time."

"Yes, I know, it's just… I don't know. Something felt…off."

"I'm sure it's nothing. Now come on. We're here to have fun!" Chaz grabbed my hand and dragged me out on the dance floor. After shaking our tail feathers for a couple of songs, Josette slipped away backstage while the band played on. I watched her walk, light and delicate, across the stage, envying her slim figure in that slinky dress.

A few minutes later, or at least I assumed it was a few minutes, she returned, hovering at the side of the stage as unobtrusively as possible. The sax player tapped the trumpeter and then left the stage to join Josette. They bent their heads together a moment before he disappeared backstage, leaving Josette to make her way to the bar.

A few moments later, the sax player returned clutching a cigarette and a lighter in one hand, the other thrust into the pocket of his black jacket. He strode across the dance floor and exited out the door leading to the front stairs. He looked more like a man on a mission than one headed for a smoke. Maybe he didn't have much time. Curiouser and curiouser.

"What's the time, Chaz?" I bellowed in his ear over the music.

"Quarter past one or so. Why?"

"I do believe it's cocktail time." I was feeling a pleasant buzz and didn't want to risk it wearing off.

We'd just reached our table when there was a slight pause in the music. I heard a faint popping sound. It sounded familiar, but I couldn't place it at first. "Did you hear that?" I asked as I slid into the booth.

"Hear what, old bean?" Chaz asked, taking a seat.

I frowned, recalling where I'd heard it before. Felix and his friends off to hunt grouse. "It sounded like a gunshot, but very quiet. Muffled, perhaps."

"'Fraid not. Probably a cork. Loads of champers in here, don't you know."

I glanced around. The barkeep was in the middle of shaking a cocktail. I couldn't see anyone else with a fresh bottle of champagne. I shook off the odd feeling. Maybe he was right. Or maybe I was imagining things. Too many highballs. Or maybe not enough.

The waiter arrived with fresh drinks as the saxophonist reappeared looking a little jittery. I guess the ciggy hadn't worked. He quickly took his place, rejoining the music as if nothing had happened. Was it just me, or were his hands shaking a bit?

The piece came to an end, and the master of ceremonies popped up on stage. "Ladies and gentlemen, please welcome back Josette Margaux."

Josette left her drink at the bar and tripped lightly across the stage to take her place. She smiled at the audience, but I could have sworn she looked strained. She opened her mouth.

A piercing scream rent the air.

Chapter 7

Everyone froze, eyes glued to the backstage curtains. Another scream. I jumped up from the table.

"Darling, where are you going?" Chaz demanded, half rising.

"Someone's in trouble." I strode toward the door leading backstage. Since I'd used the WC the evening before, I was familiar with the layout.

"Dash it, Ophelia!" Chaz shouted, running after me. "Let someone else handle it."

I ignored him, pushing my way through the door. Down the short hall past the WC, I found a door standing open. Inside, sprawled across a desk in a pool of blood, was Alfred Musgrave with a bullet hole in the back of his head. And over him stood Helena, white as a ghost, her heavy makeup smeared by tears.

"I-I think he's dead," she sobbed. Her voice was hoarse from screaming.

"It would appear that way," I said dryly.

I have no idea why I didn't do something proper like faint. Any normal upper crust woman would do so and gracefully. Preferably into the arms of a delightfully gorgeous peer of the realm. Maybe it was my practical upbringing, or working in a hospital during the War. Or maybe it was dealing with Lord R's death. But somehow, I marshalled my inner strength and took charge.

"Chaz." I whirled to face my friend. "Call the police immediately. Not from in here." There were spatters of blood across the rotor. "There must be another phone. Helena? Helena!"

She jerked a little as if I'd pulled her out of a day dream. "Behind the bar."

"Ophelia, there's obviously a killer on the loose. I'm not leaving you," he protested.

I gave him a look. "An even better reason for you to get the police here quickly."

Chaz nodded and hurried out. Good man.

"Helena stop sniveling." Her whimpers were getting on my nerves. Honestly, the woman needed to grow a spine. "You." I snapped at the reedy man who had appeared in the doorway, eyes wide behind round rimmed glasses. "Who are you?"

He swallowed, massive Adam's apple bobbing wildly. "John Bamber, My Lady. Club manager."

"Put someone to guard the door. Then get Mrs. Fairfax a stiff drink," I ordered.

He dipped his head like a stork and scurried off to do my bidding. I wondered vaguely if he could have done it, but I was too concerned about Helena's state of mind and the preservation of the crime scene to worry about it just then. I knew from my obsession with crime novels that many clues could be found in a scene such as this.

I'd learned from Aunt Butty that acting like one was in charge was a sure-fire way to get others to believe one was in charge. Unfortunately, now that I was in charge, I wasn't sure what to do. Probably I should stay put, but natural curiosity got the better of me.

Edging closer to the body, I eyeballed the scene. Musgrave had been sitting at Helena's desk, back to the door, apparently writing something, as a pen was still clutched in one hand. The document itself must be beneath him. Too bad. I'd have liked to take a gander at it before the police arrived.

A few items were scattered about—papers and whatnot—as if there'd been a bit of a tussle. Except that Musgrave was completely unruffled. I wondered how that could be. Had he been in a fight with someone before sitting down? Or, perhaps, there'd been a struggle between two other people while he sat there writing. Far-fetched as that might be.

I eyed the scene carefully. Dangling from a chain attached to Musgrave's trousers was a pocket watch. The face had been smashed and little bits of glass littered the rose and gold Turkish carpet. I frowned. The hands had stopped at twenty minutes past one.

"The coppers are on their way," Chaz announced from the doorway.

I stepped back and realized my foot had been covering a small, white feather. An unusual place for such a thing. I picked it up and inspected it. It was the sort of feather that was used to stuff pillows, but there wasn't a pillow in sight.

The manager arrived with a finger of whiskey which he urged on Helena Fairfax. I wished I had asked for a glass for myself. Absentmindedly, I tucked the feather away in my evening bag.

"Mr., ah..." His name had escaped me entirely.

"John Bamber, m'lady." The manager swallowed. I once again noted his prominent Adam's apple bobbing up and down.

"Mr. Bamber, would you be so kind as to take Mrs. Fairfax somewhere less..." I waved vaguely at the body. "She shouldn't be seeing this. But stick close. The police will no doubt have questions." Not that I'd been involved with the police before. When Felix died it had been natural causes and the doctor had signed the certificate without another thought. No police involvement necessary. During my time at the hospital I was dealing with soldiers wounded in battle, not through nefarious means. Still, it seemed logical that the police would want to question everyone. Just like in my favorite Hercule Poirot novels.

"Yes, of course." John Bamber placed a solicitous hand on Helena's arm. "Mrs. Fairfax, why don't you come with me." She allowed him to lead her like a lamb from the room.

"What time is it?" I asked Chaz, eyes still locked on the watch.

"Half past one. Why?"

I frowned. "Something's off. I know I was a bit fuzzy, but remember I thought heard a shot at one? That must have been the shot that killed him, right?"

"So it would seem."

"But the watch was smashed at twenty past, which is a mere ten minutes ago."

"Likely when he was killed," Chaz said. "The shot you thought you heard was probably something else."

"Maybe, but how did the watch get smashed?"

Chaz tucked his hands in his pockets. "A struggle perhaps. There's stuff everywhere."

I shook my head. "But there are no signs of a struggle on the body. No defense wounds. He's just sitting there, shot."

"Let the police handle it, old thing. It's what they're paid for, am I right?"

I ignored him, my mind still working over the mystery. Nothing else appeared out of place. Other than the door, there was no other way in or out of the room. Although since the office was backstage, it was unlikely anyone would notice comings and goings during a performance.

Then there was the fact that Musgrave's back had been to the door. Anyone could have come in and shot him dead without him even realizing it. So why the fight? It was all too confusing.

There was a rustling out in the hall and a tall, gray-haired man in a dinner jacket appeared in the doorway clutching a black medical bag. "I heard there was need of a doctor?"

Chaz gave him a suspicious glare. "Who told you that?"

"Mr. Bamber, the manager. He came to fetch me. Doctor Charles Eliot, at your service."

"I'm afraid you can't help him, Doctor," I said, motioning to the very dead Alfred Musgrave.

"Oh, dear." He strode across the carpet and took Musgrave's wrist between his fingers. "Yes, quite dead, I'm afraid. By at least half an hour, I'd say." He straightened, shaking his head. "Do you know who killed him?"

"Unfortunately, not," I admitted. "I'm guessing Mr. Bamber wanted your help with Mrs. Fairfax. She was a bit... out of sorts."

"Ah, yes. Point the way."

Chaz ushered him out of the room. I wasn't sure what else to do, so I took a seat on a comfortable looking armchair in the corner. I assumed it was for visitors, or perhaps so Helena would be more comfortable while doing her books—or whatever it was the owner of a nightclub did.

It was a cozy sort of room, if you discounted the body. Feminine without being over-the-top ruffles and nonsense. The Turkish carpet, which covered most of the floor, was plush and expensive, the chair on which I sat upholstered to match it. The modern walnut desk—shoved against the back wall—currently hosting the dead man was elegantly curved with delicate legs and a number of drawers with crystal pulls. Along one wall were several cabinets, no doubt containing various documents pertaining to business. A sleek pendant light hung from precisely the middle of the ceiling, and the corner opposite me contained a large ficus tree, giving the room a less severe air.

I must have waited a good ten minutes or more before there was another bustling out in the hall, followed by the murmur of masculine voices. Then a man strode into the room.

He was of medium height, medium build, medium looks, and medium coloring. One of those absolutely forgettable people. Except for his eyes. They were hard, cold, and saw far too much. His stare made me vaguely uncomfortable.

He reached into the breast pocket of his suit and pulled out a warrant card. "Detective Inspector North, Scotland Yard. I hear there's been a murder."

"Lady Rample. And, yes, as you can see." I pointed rather dramatically.

"You discovered the body?" His gaze was sharp.

"No. That was Helena. Mrs. Fairfax. I heard her scream and came to help."

"How kind of you." His tone dripped with sarcasm.

"Listen, mister…"

"Thank you, Lady Rample. That will be all."

"I can help, you know," I said, refusing to be dismissed that easily.

"I don't need interfering busybodies poking their noses into my business. You can wait outside. If I have any questions, I'll have one of my men fetch you." And with that rather rude proclamation, he firmly turned his back on me.

"How ghastly," Aunt Butty said calmly as if I'd told her I'd been stung by a bee. She refilled my tea from her gold and turquoise Royal Daulton teapot. "That police detective sounds like a dreadful bore."

"Well, yes." I was a little surprised she wasn't more horrified by the murder. Or the fact I was one of the people that found the body. But then, Aunt Butty wasn't one to be upset by things that shocked other people. One of her finer qualities that I seem to have had the good fortune to inherit. "I admit to harboring violence in my heart when he wouldn't listen to me."

I'd tried to tell him about the watch situation. That the timing was off, but he shooed me away, telling me to go enjoy myself. Which made me want to tell him what he could do to *himself*. But as I was raised in a vicarage and felt that prison wouldn't suit, I'd managed to bite my tongue. Just barely.

"Do you know, he even called me an interfering busybody." Then he'd bustled about ordering his men to get finger dabs and puffing his chest out importantly until I got annoyed—not to mention bored—and decided to retreat. Perhaps Chaz could get some juicy tidbits out of Helena.

"Shocking. Did you at least find out what it was this Musgrave person was writing?" Aunt Butty had a curiosity problem as big as mine.

"Yes." I leaned forward to drop sugar lumps in my tea. "The ladies' powder room is a perfect spot for eavesdropping. Turns out, the note was dated at the top and the time placed next to it."

"How strange. One doesn't usually note the time on one's correspondence. What else did it say?"

I shrugged and leaned back, teacup in hand. I took a sip. It was a bit bitter. "It was addressed to Helena Fairfax. It said he couldn't wait any longer and had to leave, but that he needed to talk to her about something of importance. Which is dashed odd since I heard them the night before talking about an audit. They'd already set up the time and Helena was there, at the club. Why would he be waiting?"

"The whole thing sounds strange to me," Aunt Butty said. She took a sip of her own tea and made a face. "I really must find a decently trained girl. This one can't even brew a proper pot of tea. I mean, really, how hard can it be?" She rang the bell, her wide sleeves fluttering wildly.

Today she was dressed in a simple, cream-colored shift dress. Very classic. Very not my aunt. However, over it she wore a black silk robe embroidered with Chinese dragons and trimmed in cream fringe. She wore it open like a normal person might wear a cardigan. And instead of proper shoes, she wore red mules with little tufts of feathers dyed to match. Her iron gray hair had been twisted in a knot on top her head and stabbed through with red chopsticks from which swung little gold dragons. She wore matching gold dragon earrings which dangled from her lobes, and a dragon dress pin, also gold, but with little rubies for eyes. Now *that* was very much my aunt.

"I am curious," I said, finally veering toward the subject that had been bothering me, "does Helena Fairfax have the same drug problem as her husband?"

Butty's eyes widened. "Goodness. Not that I've heard. What do you know?" She leaned forward eagerly.

"I'm not certain," I admitted. "But I ran into her the other day and she looked a bit glassy-eyed. I thought perhaps she was on something."

"Perhaps she was nipping at the bottle," Aunt Butty said. "Sampling her wares, that sort of thing."

"I suppose." But I had a feeling it was more than that.

The door to the sitting room opened and a mousy woman popped her head in. "Whotcha, miss?"

My aunt rolled her eyes dramatically. "Do you see what I put up with?"

"I'm surprised you haven't fired her," I muttered over my teacup, trying to hide a smile. Especially given how she criticized my own maid, but Aunt Butty had a soft spot for the impossible. Which is no doubt why she took me on way-back-when.

"Flora," my aunt said imperiously, her nose angled just so, "you have over brewed the tea again."

Flora blinked, her narrow face drooping into an expression of abject blankness. "Over brewed?"

"Yes. It's bitter."

"Me mum says wot I got ter get all the goodness outta it."

Aunt Butty rubbed between her eyes. "Be that as it may, in this house we brew the tea for precisely three minutes. No more. No less. Is that understood?"

"Sure, miss. You want I should brew it again?"

"Never mind." Aunt Butty heaved a sigh. "We shall make do."

Flora beamed. "Sure 'nuff. Hey, whatsit about some toff getting hisself offed at the club?" I assumed she referred to Musgrave, though he could hardly be considered a toff.

Aunt Butty's expression hardened. "Were you listening at the door again?"

"Well, hard not to, ain't it? 'Sides, my cousin works there."

My ears perked right up. "Does she?"

Flora turned her squinty gaze to me. "Aye, Miss, that she does."

"My Lady, Flora," Aunt Butty corrected in a tone of long suffering.

"Wotcher, miss?"

This time Aunt Butty massaged her temple. "Never mind."

"Go on, Flora," I encouraged, not at all worried about being called "miss" instead of by my title. "What does your cousin do at the club?"

"She's a dresser, miss. Well, that's what she does now, see. She dresses for that new singer. When she ain't serving drinks or whatnot."

Aunt Butty and I exchanged glances. "How interesting." I eyed her casually over the rim of my cup. "I imagine she hears all sorts of interesting things."

"You betcha, miss. I mean, My Lady. You never would believe what she done tol' me the other night." She leaned forward, eyes wide as if about to impart great wisdom. "That fancy singer lady wot she dresses for? She been getting it on with one of them musicians, iffen you know what I mean."

Unfortunately, I did. I also felt an odd flutter. Was the pianist sleeping with one of the singers? "I don't suppose you know which musician?"

"No, miss... Milady. But it be the musician wot's also getting it on with the lady wot owns the place."

Chapter 8

"Good God, don't tell me Helena is having an affair with one of her musicians. How scandalous." Chaz didn't sound scandalized in the least. In fact, he sounded like a giddy schoolboy. The man loved a chinwag more than any woman I knew. Actually, come to think of it, you could say that about most men. Lord R had been a grand one for gossip. "I don't suppose you know which musician?" He eyed me with a knowing look which I ignored.

"I don't. Which is why I'm going to talk to Helena."

"You can't go barging in, demanding to know the sordid details of her love life. Really, old thing, it isn't done."

I snorted delicately. "As if that ever stopped you." Chaz was an incorrigible gossip, the juicier the better. Especially when bedroom hijinks were involved.

He paused to think it over. "Fair point. But men are different, you understand."

"If you mean men are allowed to act like floozies while women are branded floozies for wearing too short dresses, then yes, I am familiar." My tone was tart.

"It's a bit early in the day," he continued, as I pulled up to the Astoria Club door with a screech. "The place doesn't open for hours."

"It's late afternoon. I'm sure she's cleaning up or doing paperwork or whatever it is club owners do." After their partners are murdered. Helena hadn't struck me as the sort to spend the day crying at home. Especially as she clearly hadn't cared for Musgrave.

I wondered what she would do now. Go out into the open, reveal her dirty secret to the world? Surely not. Perhaps she'd find another business partner. Who inherited Alfred Musgrave's share? Would they take over?

I slammed the car door and strode across the pavement toward the unmarked door. Chaz trotted along behind, silent, but exuding a sort of upper crust distaste for the whole business. The man loved a good lark... until it became *too* sordid. I feared I was skirting the edges.

The door swung open easily, allowing us entry into the belly of the beast, so to speak. It was strange to find it empty, quiet. A dark, expectant hush as if waiting for life to refill it. The musicians' platform cast eerie shadows, and I wondered again which one of them Helena was sleeping with.

Since no one was out front, we made our way to the back. Helena's office where Musgrave had been murdered was locked up tight, but a light shone from the room next to it. I popped my head in to find Helena had taken up residence next door in what was clearly a storage room. A small table had been shoved up against a rack of glassware and Helena hunched over it, scribbling in a ledger, a pillow tucked neatly behind her back. I knocked softly and she nearly jumped a foot.

"Lady Rample! And Chaz. Whatever are you doing here?" Her face was paler than usual, dark circles etched beneath her eyes. If I was a betting woman, I'd take odds she hadn't slept a wink. Most likely had another drink or three, as well.

"Call me Ophelia, please. We came to check up on you after that ghastly business." The lie slipped easily off my tongue. A little too easily, perhaps. I got used to it during the War, lying to soldiers, telling them they'd be alright when I knew they wouldn't. Comfort trumped truth back then. But that was long ago in another life. I assured myself that, once again, lies were necessary if I was going to play detective.

She shook her head and closed the ledger, leaving a pencil to mark her spot. "It's dreadful, isn't it?"

"I'm a little surprised to find you here. You must be quite upset."

"The show must go on," she said, rather dramatically. "I can't… Closing for even one night is impossible, you see."

"And the police didn't force you to close?" Chaz asked.

"That detective person agreed to let us open as long as the crime scene remained locked." She shuddered. "Crime scene. Such a terrible thought. I can't believe someone would murder poor Musgrave."

"Can't you?" I asked dryly.

Twin pink spots burned in her alabaster cheeks. "Very well. I *can* imagine someone wanted to murder the man. He was such a boor. Very unkind. But one doesn't go about *saying* such things, does one?"

"Of course not," Chaz said bracingly. I could almost feel him willing me to be more sympathetic with Helena.

We both ignored him. "Chaz, why don't you go get Helena a drink?"

"It's the middle of the day," he protested. As if that ever stopped him.

"She's going to need it," I said firmly.

There was a pause, and then he trudged out muttering things under his breath about busybodies and nonsense.

"I assume this means we're going to have a rather serious discussion." Her tone gave nothing away.

There was nowhere for me to sit, so I leaned casually against the wall. Very unladylike. "I had a chat with one of your employees." I wasn't going to tell her which one if I didn't have to. Costing a woman her job in the midst of a recession wasn't on my to-do list. Mabel had only been trying to help, so I would protect her as long as I could.

A small frown line marred her otherwise perfectly smooth forehead. "Did you? Why?"

"I heard a rumor that I wanted confirmed."

She lifted a perfectly penciled brow. "A rumor? How ghastly. What rumor?"

I eyed her a moment, letting the silence stretch until it made the skin on the back of my neck itch. "Which musician?"

Helena didn't pretend not to know what I was talking about. "Oh, don't worry, it's not the pianist." She smiled. "I saw the way you looked at Hale. You want me to make an introduction?"

"Maybe." My heart rate sped up a little. Ridiculous organ. "Did you also know that *your* musician is sleeping with one of the singers?"

"I had my suspicions." Her expression was tight, lips pinched, which told me she wasn't pleased about the news.

"Did Musgrave know?" Maybe that's why somebody offed him.

"Unlikely. The man had eyes for two things: money and women. Very *young* women. I'm afraid I'm far too old for the likes of him."

"And the singer?"

"That's another matter. They're both fairly young. I suppose he might have been interested in one. Or both."

"Maybe he tried to steal her away? From the musician, I mean. Got himself killed?"

She shrugged. "Unlikely. Alfred would have simply had the man beat up. He was into that sort of thing, you know. Very distasteful." Her expression had the cast of one who'd just sucked on a lemon.

"Do tell."

"Last year he was gaga over some chanteuse from Café du Paris. He wooed her into his bed and convinced her to leave Café du Paris and join our club, but the club owner wouldn't let her out of her contract. Alfred hired a few unsavories to beat the man up."

"Did she come to the Astoria after that?" I asked.

Helena's smirk had a hard, brittle edge to it. "Unfortunately for Alfred, it upset the poor thing so much, that she took a train back to Liverpool the next day. Not that I blame her."

"No, indeed." It hadn't escaped me that she'd dodged the question of which musician she was sleeping with. But, as they say, there are more ways than one to skin a cat. I switched subjects. "Is it possible for me to talk to Mabel."

"Why ever for? The police seem to have a handle on things."

"Trust me. Looks can be deceiving," I said wryly.

She gave a rather Gallic one-shoulder shrug. "Do as you please. She's down the hall. I've got more important things to worry about. Like keeping this club running."

I turned to go, then hesitated. Turning back, I said, "Helena, what happens to Musgrave's half of the club now he's dead?"

"Oh, that's easy. It reverts to me. He had no heirs, you see, other than some half-sister in America. I don't think he cared for her. Our lawyers set it up so if I died, he got my half and vice versa."

"Is that usual?" Seemed a strange way to run a business, but then, I'd never run one before. Perhaps Chaz would know.

"No idea. Now, really, I must get on," she said tiredly. "Alfred's death has left me in such a bind. I'm up to here in paperwork."

"But of course." As I rose, she turned her back, shuffling through several files.

Figuring that was all I'd get out of her for the moment, I exited her temporary office and met Chaz in the hall, a tumbler of amber liquid in one hand.

"How'd you get on?" he asked.

"Tell you later," I said, keeping my voice low. "I'm off to talk to the dresser, Mabel. You go give Helena her drink and try and get what you can out of her."

"What makes you think she'll tell *me* anything?"

I gave him a look. "Use your charm. It's quite devastating when you want it to be."

He perked up. "So true."

"By the by, is it common practice for one business partner to inherit the other's half if they die? Rather than the family, I mean?"

"It's not uncommon, particularly in America. Why?"

"Tell you later." I dismissed him, vaguely disappointed the whole setup wasn't more sinister.

"Meet you at the bar after." And he slipped into the room, closing the door behind him. I strode off to find Mabel.

I found Mabel in what I assumed was the singers' dressing room. Apparently, they didn't get their own. Instead it was a long, narrow room with a low ceiling. On the far end was a dressing screen set up next to a rack of costumes. Against the long wall next to the door was a fainting couch piled high with more clothing. Across from me were three small vanities, mirrors lined in bright bulbs. The middle vanity was empty, but the two outside ones were filled with makeup and lotions and feathers and whatnot.

The vanity on the left was tidy with a large pot of wrinkle cream and a faded photo of a young couple in their best clothing. A wedding photo, perhaps? I wasn't close enough to make out their faces. The right-hand vanity was a disaster of perfumes, jewelry, and tubes of lipstick. A large vase of pink, hot house roses sat precariously on the edge. A stack of cheap novels was crammed next to it, the one on top the latest by Agatha Christie. The same one I was reading.

A short, plump woman of indeterminate middle age in a baggy, gray dress was sorting through the pile making *tut tutting* sounds. She glanced up as I knocked on the door frame.

"Yes, madam? May I help you?" Her tone was polite, with a thread of 'you don't belong here' running beneath it. She may look sweet and auntie-like, but I had no doubt she was capable of beating off an intruder should the need arise. There was something oddly fearsome about her.

"Lady Rample. My aunt's maid is your cousin, Flora."

A smile creased Mabel's face and she dropped the slip she'd been holding onto the pile. "Oh, so sorry, m'lady. I didn't realize. It was ever so kind of your aunt to give Flora a position. The poor girl isn't..." She hesitated as if uncertain how to proceed.

"Isn't a typical lady's maid," I supplied without rancor.

She chuckled. "Aye, you've got that right, m'lady. Now how may I be of service to your ladyship?"

"Whose dressing table is that?" I asked, nodding to the one with the roses and novels. I wasn't sure why, but I was curious to know which of the singers was a mystery fan. Seemed like it might be important, though goodness knows how.

"That's that fancy girl's. One from France. Josette."

Interesting. I hadn't pegged her as a mystery reader, but you never know about people. "You know about the trouble last night?"

"My, yes. Terrible business. Is it true he was shot in the back?"

"Unfortunately, yes. Back of the head, actually. He tried to fight them off, too," I lied. I doubted Musgrave had done any such thing. "His pocket watch was smashed."

"He was that obsessed with that thing. Always checking the time. Flashing it about like it were somethin' special." She picked up the slip again and carefully folded it. She glanced furtively around me as if to make certain no one had followed me in. "Not that I was that surprised, mind you. About the killing."

I lifted a brow. "Oh?"

"That Mr. Musgrave weren't exactly a gentleman, if you know what I mean, m'lady."

"I have an idea. Was there... anyone *specific* who might have had a motive?"

"Well, I don't know as to that, but that poor girl, Josette? He weren't exactly shy about putting his hands where he shouldn't. New, she is. Shiny. And when he couldn't get to her, well, there was Coco, now, wasn't there?"

"Surely their husbands or boyfriends objected."

She gave me a sideways look. "Coco, she's married to that one what plays the funny horn thing."

I pondered what that meant. "The saxophone?"

"Yes, that one."

Perhaps the saxophonist took out Musgrave for dallying with his wife. Then again, I'd seen him leave the club for a cigarette break with my own eyes. "What about Josette?"

"The two of 'em been running around since she got here. Her and that funny horn player. But they gotta keep it quiet, see, because the musician is married to that Coco and Himself brought Josette over from Paree for the express purpose of..." She turned a little red. "Well, I'm sure you can imagine."

"Rather." What a right tosser that Musgrave was. If he wasn't dead, I might have rung his neck myself. "So, you think the saxophonist might have killed Musgrave?"

"Doubt it. Would have been more like Musgrave would have killed *him* iffen he'd found out about the two of them. Probably killed her, too. Or shipped her back to France."

As I made my way to the bar, I pondered what Mabel told me. On the one hand, it opened up a plethora of suspects. On the other hand, at least two of them had been on stage the night Musgrave was killed. I couldn't see how they could have pulled it off.

Chaz was waiting for me, drink in hand. "You'll never believe what happened, Old Bean. The musician confessed!"

Shéa MacLeod

Chapter 9

Dr. Eliot kept offices on Harley Street. Well, technically just off Harley Street. Close enough he could claim he had offices in that elevated area, far enough that the rents weren't so exorbitant.

His secretary—a spare, angular woman about my own age—opened the glossy black door marked with a brass "42" and gave me the once-over. "Have you an appointment?"

Her voice had the carefully modulated tones of the upper classes, but with the slightly flat undertone of someone who hadn't set foot in London until she was an adult. I was guessing she'd been born in the Midlands and to a lower-class family, no doubt, and had bettered herself through elocution and education. I had to admit I approved. I always admired a woman who pullled herself up by her bootstraps, as those brawny Americans say.

"No appointment," I admitted cheerfully. "However, I'm certain the good doctor will see me. Lady Rample."

The woman didn't blink as she stared down her angular nose. "He's busy."

"It's about the murder."

This time her eyes did widen a fraction, although she quickly hid her reaction. "You'd better come in." She swung the door open and ushered me into a narrow entry. "Wait here." She slammed the door and disappeared down the hall and through a door, her sensible heels clicking smartly on the black and white tiles.

"Well, send her in!" I recognized the stentorian voice of the doctor.

The secretary reappeared and pointed me down the hall before departing for some other part of the house without a word. Shame. I could really use a cup of tea right about now. Preferably with a splash of medicinal whiskey.

I found the doctor seated behind the desk of a typical doctor's office. A potted fern sat in one corner, multiple certificates and licenses in silver frames graced the walls, and a shelf of medical texts leaned precariously next to a window overlooking a miniscule garden. A willow tree neatly framed the outside of the window, its soft, green leaves still unfurling from winter sleep.

"Lady Rample," the doctor boomed, standing slightly. "Please sit. What can I do for you?"

I took a seat so that he could sit, too. "Dr. Eliot, thank you for seeing me. I wanted to speak to you about the death of Mr. Musgrave."

"Nasty business, that. Terrible."

"Yes," I murmured. "I heard that the saxophone player admitted to the deed."

His eyebrows rose. "Did he? Dashed odd, these foreigners."

"Well, it's all very strange, don't you think? The note, for one. Don't you think the fact that he wrote the time at the top was... unusual?"

"Ah, the note. I saw that, too. Yes, I agree. I sometimes am required to note times in my note taking for patient files, but in a personal note? Unusual at the least." His confirmation was satisfying.

"Then there was the pocket watch."

"Smashed, yes. The detective was quite thrilled. Proof of time of death. In a way."

"What do you mean?"

He harrumphed. "Well, I don't mean to speak out of turn, but according to the watch, the victim was killed at twenty past one. However," he leaned forward, hands clasped on the desk top, "I inspected the body at one forty-five, which would have been a mere fifteen minutes after the supposed death. Which is impossible. Musgrave was dead much longer than that. As I said at the time, at least thirty minutes. Temperature, you know."

"I assume you informed Detective North," I said. The doctor seemed the conscientious type.

He snorted. "Of course, but D.I. North isn't exactly a listening sort. I think he's decided that the pocket watch is the final word. And, after all, I'm not an official police physician. He doesn't consider me the sort of 'expert' he should listen to."

I sank back down, remembering the brusque detective. "Fair point." I mulled it over a moment. "Perhaps he'll listen to someone else."

The doctor lifted a brow. "What do you mean?"

"Someone in a position of authority. Someone with a bit of power behind him." A male someone. Preferably with a title and a pocketful of connections.

"Have you any suggestions?"

Chaz was the first to come to mind, but alas Chaz was more charm. Less battle-axe. "I have an idea, yes. Meet me at the police station tomorrow. Nine sharp. We'll make that detective listen."

"I can't believe you talked me into this," Aunt Butty said, adjusting her hat. It was a felt cloche in flamingo pink with a gaudy diamond pin the size of a tea saucer from which sprouted half a dozen pink feathers in varying shapes and sizes. In style, it was about as close to modern fashion as could be expected from my aunt, but it was as startlingly hideous as the rest of her head gear.

In front of us loomed the Gothic ramparts of the London home of Lord Varant. Frankly, the place needed a face lift. It was the perfect setting for some cheap Hollywood horror. There was sure to be a body plastered behind a wall in the library or buried beneath the floorboards in the wine cellar.

We were ushered into the parlor by Lord Varant's very proper butler where we made ourselves as comfortable as possible on the most dashedly uncomfortable furniture imaginable. I was certain most of it dated back to Queen Victoria's reign, if not further. The room smelled of lemon and wax, a sure sign that the maids paid attention to the room, if no one else did.

At last, Lord Varant put in an appearance. "Ladies, to what do I owe this pleasure?"

Aunt Butty held out her hand and posed dramatically. "Varant. So lovely to see you again. Thank you for seeing us. Ophelia has a small matter she wishes to discuss with you."

Varant's lip curled in amusement as he bowed over my aunt's hand. "Of course." He turned to greet me, a smoldering heat in his gaze. I wasn't entirely sure whether it displeased me or not. "Lady Rample." He bowed over my hand, but there was no amusement, only that smoldering heat, turned up several notches. "Pleasure." There was a wealth of meaning in that one word.

I cleared my throat. "Lord Varant—" Might as well get right down to it before I did something unladylike.

"Just Varant, please."

"Very well." I might have blushed a little, which was silly. Calling him simply Varant indicated a certain level of intimacy. "I need your help."

"Anything." He meant it.

I was well aware of my powers over Varant. His solicitousness during Aunt Butty's party had proven that.

Not to mention our history, such as it was. Varant took a seat directly opposite me, neatly crossing one leg over the other. His trouser legs were pleated to a knife edge and his shoes shined so thoroughly I could have no doubt seen my reflection in them. "Now, how may I be of assistance?"

"I have a meeting tomorrow morning at Scotland Yard," I blurted.

If he was shocked, he gave no indication. "How interesting."

I quickly explained about the murder, the watch, and the saxophonist's likely false confession. "So, you see, I must remind the detective in charge of all of this, and convince him that the musician has made a false confession."

"I see." He appeared to mull it over. "What I do not see is how I can be of assistance."

"You know the police commissioner, I believe," Aunt Butty said.

Varant raised a saturnine brow. "He's a member of my club, yes."

"Well, this detective is a bit of a... well, he's not going to listen to a woman, is he? So I was hoping you would come with me tomorrow and help me speak to him. Maybe then he'll listen." It goaded me to have to ask a man's help, but I wasn't stupid. I might be a modern, independent woman, but the rest of the world had yet to catch up. Men like Detective Inspector North were firmly rooted in the past and preferred to stay that way.

.

Varant smiled as if he knew exactly what I was thinking. "What time?"

"Nine sharp."

"That's quite early for you."

"Needs must," I said firmly. I'd just have to skip the jazz club tonight. More's the pity. I'd been rather looking forward to another bout of flirting with Hale Davis. But our introductions would have to wait. "Will you help me?"

Varant gave a quick nod. "I'll see you tomorrow."

Shéa MacLeod

Chapter 10

The next morning found myself, Varant, and Dr. Eliot sitting in front of Detective Inspector North's banged up pinewood desk while the detective glowered at us over his pipe. The sweet smoke drifted through the air leaving behind a bluish haze that tickled my nose. The sun glimmered through a small window, lighting up dust motes that danced in its rays. The detective clearly didn't find this nearly as magical as I did.

There were squint lines around his eyes as if he needed glasses, and his nose was slightly bulbous. Beneath it was a ridiculously tiny moustache the same medium brown as his hair.

"The Yard thanks you for your assistance, Lady Rample, but I really don't see—"

"That's the problem, isn't it?" I snapped, thoroughly exasperated. We'd already been at this a good ten minutes at the least. "You *don't* see what is plainly in front of your face."

Varant laid his hand over mine in an attempt to still my runaway mouth. "What Lady Rample means—"

"Lady Rample can speak for herself, thank you." My tone was arch. I was beginning to wonder why I'd brought him along in the first place. Oh, yes. He knew the police commissioner which was the only reason North was entertaining me at all. I drew in a steadying breath. "Detective Inspector North, I feel duty bound to bring to your attention a couple of items which I'm *sure* you noticed yourself, but which I wouldn't be able to sleep at night if I didn't ensure I passed them along to you."

North rubbed his forehead as though he wished for headache powders. "Go on."

I cleared my throat, giving Varant a smug look. "Yesterday I spoke with Doctor Eliot, here." I gave the doctor a nod. He smiled back nervously. I don't think he liked being in the presence of the acerbic detective.

North glared at me, teeth clenching the stem of his pipe. "Why would you bother the good doctor?"

"I wanted to make sure I had all the facts, of course."

He grimaced. "What facts are those?"

"Well, I understand that the saxophonist has admitted to murdering Mr. Musgrave."

"Yes, that's correct."

I shook my head. "Actually, it isn't."

North eyeballed me in restrained amusement. Clearly, he assumed I was a rich aristocrat with nothing better to do but meddle in his affairs. Which was only partially true. I hadn't been born rich or an aristocrat, and I could probably find something else to do if I set my mind to it. "Come again?"

"I happened to notice at the, er, crime scene that Mr. Musgrave's pocket watch was smashed, alerting you to the exact time of death." I eyed him carefully. He didn't blink.

"Yes. Twenty minutes past one o'clock."

"But I spoke to the dresser at the club. Mabel. She says that—"

"Really, Lady Rample. You should leave such matters to the police."

"It's only that—"

"I really haven't time for this, Lady Rample. I appreciate that your friend here," North shot a glare at Varant, "knows the Commissioner, but I'm in the middle of an investigation."

"Sir! She's confessed, sir!" A ruddy-cheeked young uniformed police man with a moon face and a head of wild, strawberry curls popped his head in the door and beamed excitedly at North.

"What's the meaning of this, Higgins?" North barked.

"The singer down at the jazz club, sir. She's only gone and confessed to the murder."

"Coco Starr?" I asked in astonishment. Had Coco confessed to protect her husband?

"No, ma'am. Josette something," Higgins said.

"That's impossible. The sax player did it." North was scowling hard enough I thought his face might break. Which would have been no great pity. "She's lying to cover for him. I'll bet my last farthing."

No doubt he was right. Josette was probably trying to protect her lover. Which was unnecessary since he hadn't done anything.

"Maybe Lady Rample should ask her," Varant suggested.

North looked affronted. "Lady Rample?"

"This singer may not talk to a man, but women like to share gossip and whatnot," Varant said languidly before winking at me. If it hadn't been for the wink, I might have boshed him over the head for maligning my sex.

"It's true," I joined in. "I'm sure she'll be much more likely to talk to another woman."

"Other than confessing, she wouldn't say another word, sir. The lady may be right," Higgins supplied helpfully, which earned him a glare from North.

"Very well," the DI said at last. "Lady Rample, you may help me question the… suspect." He said the last word almost as if it should be in quotes. Clearly, he didn't think Josette was any more guilty than I did.

The small room was painted a dull greenish-gray suitable for military installations and insane asylums. A narrow window high in the wall let in the tiniest amount of light. A single, scarred wooden table sat in the middle of the room. Josette Margaux perched ramrod straight in her chair, her red lips pressed into a firm line as if to keep them from trembling. She wore a simple linen day dress the color of pale cream which offset her dusky, golden skin and smooth, black hair. She glanced up, dark eyes wide, as I entered behind the Detective Inspector.

He held out one of the two chairs across from Josette, so I could sit before taking the other. I barely heard DI North as he cautioned her. Instead, I watched her face closely. She looked a little ashen and pinched. Beneath her carefully powdered face there were dark circles under her eyes. She looked a decade older than when I'd last seen her.

"Please repeat again what you told my Sergeant, Miss Margeaux." DI North's voice interrupted my perusal.

She lifted her chin slightly. "I killed him."

"Alfred Musgrave?" North clarified.

"Yes." Her hands clenched tightly, the knuckles whitening. "I shot him. In the head." Her voice was light and bright with a slight French accent. Charming. Not at all suited to the grisly matter at hand.

North's expression didn't change. "At what time was this?"

"One o'clock in the morning," she said without hesitation. "After I finished singing, I walked backstage and shot him."

"Impossible," North said. "Musgrave's pocket watch was smashed at twenty minutes past one. That's when he died."

Josette's eyes widened a little, her breaths coming in quick, panicked gasps. "I-I don't know why it said that. But I shot him. I did. It's true!"

Interesting. In my experience, when someone insists with great alacrity that a thing is true, it rarely is.

"Where was the gun?" Again, North's expression was bland.

"I... had it with me."

"No, you didn't," I said.

Josette glanced at me, her mouth a tiny "o" as if she'd forgotten I was there. "But I did. I had it with me."

"On stage?" I shook my head. "Ludicrous. Where would you have kept it? Everyone was watching you."

She licked her perfectly carnelian red lips. "Under my dress."

I would have snorted, but that wouldn't have been ladylike. "Nonsense. I remember exactly what you were wearing, and believe me, you couldn't have hidden so much as a paperclip beneath that gown."

For the first time North looked amused. "Is that so?"

"Yes, Detective Inspector. It was very... form fitting. Not to mention daringly low cut, even for today's fashion."

"None the less, I killed him," Josette insisted, as if repeating it enough would make it so.

"Really?" North leaned back and crossed his arms. "What was your motive?"

"He was harassing me. Wanting me to... you know." She pressed her lips together until they formed a thin line. "I couldn't stand it anymore. So I shot him."

"Interesting," North said. "Because I think you had nothing to do with it. I think your lover shot him and you're trying to save him from hanging by muddying the waters."

"No!" She glanced at me, eyes wide and wild. "I did it. I did! It was me."

"Sorry, Josette," I said, keeping my voice gentle. "You didn't. You couldn't have. You didn't have a gun." I recalled something. "Besides, you'd already returned to the stage when I heard the shot."

North glanced at me, startled. "We'll pick this up later. Lady Rample, with me, please?" He strode from the room with me hot on his tail. In the hall he hissed, "You didn't tell me about hearing a shot."

"If you recall, I did try," I said languidly, if perhaps a little smugly. I did rather enjoy shoving it in his face. Nasty man. "However, I seem to recall you saying something insulting about meddling females." I gave him a pointed look.

He had the grace to blush. "If you would be so kind as to bring me up to speed?" The words were gritted out between clenched teeth.

"Darling, you had only to ask." I fluttered my lashes and he growled something about meddling females again, which I chose to ignore. Instead, I gave him a quick rundown of events. "I didn't realize at the time that was what it was—Chaz, that's Charles Raynott, insisted it was a champagne cork—but it had to be the shot that killed Musgrave."

"And you're sure that was after Josette returned from the dressing rooms?"

"Positive. She was sitting at the bar, drinking a glass of wine."

He nodded. "That does it. It was as I thought. The musician did it."

I shook my head. "Couldn't have."

He frowned. "What do you mean?"

"Well, he wasn't backstage, either. He'd come up front to talk to someone or other."

"You saw him up front when the shot was fired?"

I mulled it over. "No," I finally admitted. "But he wasn't backstage. He'd gone up the stairs. I lost sight of him after that. Probably went outside for a smoke."

"Damn. Oh, sorry, Lady Rample." He had the grace to look embarrassed.

I shrugged it off. "So, you see, neither one of them could possibly have done it, regardless of what they claim."

He gripped the hair on either side of his head as if he wanted to pull it out. "Then why would they confess?"

"Likely to protect each other. They're in love, you know."

"Argh! Be that as it may, I still want words with the musician."

"Can I sit in?" I asked eagerly. "After all, I'm your best witness."

He rolled his eyes. "If you must."

The saxophonist was as I remembered him: tall, thin, with skin the color of rich earth. He was probably closer to forty than thirty, but there wasn't a trace of silver in his dark hair, and while handsome, he wasn't anywhere on par with my pianist, Hale Davis. *The* pianist, I corrected myself sternly. He wasn't *my* anything.

"Beauford Parks," Detective Inspector North intoned as we took our seats across from the prisoner in a room identical to the one where we'd met Josette, "to remind you, you're still under caution. I have a few questions for you."

Parks gazed at us. His right eyelid twitched slightly. A nervous tick he couldn't hide. "I told you I killed that man. Ain't nothin' more to say." His accent was a heavy drawl. A muscle flexed in his jaw.

"Well, now, that's interesting, because Lady Rample here says you couldn't have done it," North said.

Parks glanced at me, eyes wide. "She don't know what she's talkin' about."

"If it makes you feel better, Josette didn't do it, either," I said.

North glared at me, but I ignored him. Parks wilted with relief. "Sh-she didn't? How do you know?"

I told him how I'd seen Josette go back stage. How she couldn't have had a gun on her. And how she'd been at the bar when the shot was fired. "And I know you were out front at the time of the gunshot. You couldn't have shot him either."

"But... my gun... it was missing."

North lifted a brow. "You carry a gun?"

"Sure. Can't be too careful on the road."

"Surely you don't take it on stage with you," I pointed out.

"No, ma'am. I keep it in my dressing room."

"Locked up?" North asked.

Parks scrunched his forehead. "If there's a place for it. Ain't no place for it at the Astoria Club. I stick it in the drawer of the dressing table. Nobody messes with it there. Usually."

North leaned forward, his chair creaking slightly beneath him. "So anyone could have grabbed the gun at any time?"

"Sure. Most everyone knew it was there. Made no secret of it."

Probably liked to show it off. I'd known many men who'd served in the Great War. They came in two types. The ones who wanted to forget and never discussed anything about their experiences, and those that bragged about the littlest things, showed off their weapons like they were points of pride. I was guessing Beau was the later. At least among the ladies.

North leaned back with a heavy sigh. "Great. Now we start at square one."

"You mean, you're letting me go? What about Josette?"

"Her, too," North growled. "No more lying to the police, got it?"

"Sure thing." Parks beamed a wide, white smile, filled with relief.

Back in the first interrogation room, North confronted Josette with the truth about her lies and Parks's innocence. She broke down sobbing. "I was so afraid..." she didn't finish the sentence, but neither North nor I were dummies. She'd thought her lover, Parks, had done it.

"Why did you go back stage, Josette?" I asked gently.

"Before the first set, I found a note on my dressing table. It was unsigned. It said to meet the writer back stage between sets or else he or she would tell Musgrave about Beauford Parks and me."

"So?" North asked bluntly.

"So, if Alfred found out about Beau and me, he'd have killed us both."

"You were having an affair with Musgrave," I stated, wondering how much I could get her to reveal.

"If you could call it that." Her tone was bitter. "He forced me into it. You see, I met him in Paris. He promised me the moon and stars if I came with him to London and sang in his club. The sex..." she gave a very Gallic shrug. "It just sort of happened. The price to pay, I suppose. And then he brought the band over from America and I met Beau. We fell in love, but I didn't dare break it off with Musgrave. He'd kill Beau! When I got that note... if he found out, it would have destroyed everything."

"So, you went backstage to meet the letter writer," I prompted.

She nodded. "Only, when I got there, I found Alfred dead. I thought Beau had done it. He was the only one I told about the note."

North and I exchanged glances. We both clearly had the same idea. If Josette only told Beau about the letter, there was only one other person who knew about it: the writer. And since neither Josette nor Beau killed Alfred Musgrave, naturally, the letter writer must be the killer.

"How'd things go?" Varant asked as I rejoined him in the lobby.

"Better than expected. And also, somehow worse."

"What does that mean?"

I grimaced. "We're back to square one." North would love that I included myself. "Where's the doctor?"

"He had patients. And I think he wanted to get out of here before North returned."

"Can't say I blame him. Now what?"

Varant eyed me. "Fancy a drink?"

"At this time of day? Yes, please."

Chapter 11

"So, they both confessed falsely?" Varant blew a ring of smoke toward the ceiling. Long, tapered fingers rolled the cigarette back and forth. Mesmerizing.

I managed to pull my attention back to the matter at hand. "Yes. Quite. You see, Beau—that's the saxophonist—and Josette have been having an affair ever since Musgrave brought her over from Paris. Unfortunately, there's a wrench in the works. Musgrave wants Josette to pay him in kind, if you get my meaning. And he doesn't want competition."

Varant made an expression of distaste. "Appalling behavior."

"Indeed. Not the least bit gentlemanly. Then again, Musgrave was no gentleman. In any case, after she got that mysterious note, Josette was afraid Musgrave would find out about them and kill Beau."

"She warned him."

"Naturally." I took a sip of my highball. A little on the spicy side. Still, I soldiered on. "When she found Musgrave dead backstage, she assumed Beau had done it. And when he confessed, she was sure of it. So she confessed in an attempt to save him."

"I'm assuming Beau confessed in the first place because he thought *she'd* done it."

"Exactly. He was going to confront Musgrave between sets, but apparently couldn't find him." I frowned. "Which is baffling, seeing as how Musgrave wasn't exactly hiding. He was merely in Helena's office. But whatever. The point is, the two idiots confessed in order to save each other, but it's clear that neither of them could have shot Musgrave. I heard the shot at twenty minutes past one, and Josette was already back on stage and Beau was out front." A sudden thought occurred. "You know what's odd?"

"Aside from what you've just told me, I've no idea," Varant said languidly, dangling a martini from one hand. "Do tell." He gave me that smoldering look of which he was so infamous. I ignored him, although I couldn't help the heady buzz that zinged through my body.

"Helena. She wouldn't have been late."

He blinked slowly. "Sorry. Don't follow."

"The note Musgrave wrote. He said he couldn't wait any longer, but according to his watch—which was smashed at the time of death—she was only late by perhaps five minutes. That's not that long."

Varant grew thoughtful. "No. It's not. I would have certainly waited five minutes. Longer, if it were important."

"Exactly," I said, excitement making my heart race. "He was very insistent the night before about their meeting. Why would he have given up so quickly? Besides, she was right there at the club. He could have sent the manager to get her or something. I need to see that note again."

"The police likely have it."

"I don't suppose you could pull a few strings again." The fact that Varant had so far supported my machinations only bolstered his appeal as far as I was concerned.

He smiled slowly, bedroom eyes darkening. "Perhaps."

"Here you go." North dropped the note in front of me.

"Thank you, Detective Inspector," Varant said in his perfectly proper accent. "I'll be sure to mention this to the Commissioner."

North grimaced, but didn't say anything. Smart man.

I carefully inspected the note, frowning a little as I compared the date and time to the handwriting in the note. "Detective, did you notice the time?"

"Of course. One nineteen. A minute before death." He said, clearly considered the smashed pocket watch the last word in time of death.

"But look at this." I tapped the page. "The date and the note itself... it seems different from the time. See, the numbers are thicker. A different size. And here, the date. The zeros are a bit different. Barely noticeable."

North squinted at the paper, opened his desk drawer, and drew out a magnifying glass. "By jove. You're correct." He didn't sound pleased.

"I don't think these were written by the same person."

"Nor do I," North admitted, albeit with obvious reluctance.

"It seems unusual, don't you think, that Mr. Musgrave would leave a note in the first place?" I suggested. "I mean, he and Helena were supposed to meet during the first set so he could go over the books. And clearly, he was already going over the books during the first set. Why would he write a note about being unable to wait? And then add the time, as well?"

"It is dashed strange," Varant agreed.

North mumbled something unintelligible, but it was clear to me that he was forced to agree, too. "The whole thing *is* dashed strange," he added.

"We need to talk to Mabel again," I said.

"Who the deuce is Mabel?" North demanded.

"Really, Detective Inspector, I would have thought you'd have talked to her right away. Mabel is the dresser at the club. And, in my experience, people like Mabel know everything."

Chapter 12

We found Mabel backstage at the club, ironing a gown. Her graying hair was up in a floral scarf and her cheeks were ruddy with heat. "Lady Rample!" she exclaimed when I entered her domain. I'd left the men at the bar, assuring DI North that Mabel would be more likely to talk to me than a man of the law. "You're back."

"Yes, Mabel. I need your help again." I took a seat at one of the dressing tables.

"I'll do what I can, Milady, but I'm not sure what else I can tell you." She picked up her iron again. "Hope you don't mind, but I'm on a schedule."

"Of course not. Go right ahead. Mabel, do you remember the night Musgrave died?"

"'Course, m'lady. Such a night." She shook her head and made a tutting sound as she glided the iron over layers of lemon-colored taffeta.

"Who let him in to Helena's office?"

"Why, I did, m'lady. Mrs. Fairfax was busy out front, so she gave me the key to let 'im in."

"What time was that?"

She scrunched up her nose. "Half past midnight, I reckon. He weren't no early bird. Most of 'em 'round here ain't."

"What happened after you let him in?"

"He sent me for whiskey and sommat to eat. Which I brought."

"When?"

"Ten to one. I remember 'cuz he tol' me Mrs. Fairfax was to meet him at one sharp and could I make sure she came. I tol' him where he could stick it. I got work, I do." She said the last with her nose tilted slightly in the air of one who takes pride in her work and has no time for nonsense.

"You truly told Musgrave where to, ah, 'stick it?'" I could almost imagine her doing it, too. Even if it did cost her a job.

"Well, no," she admitted. "But I thought it real hard. I did tell 'im I was busy. Like I said, I ain't got no time to waste."

"Indeed." It amused me imagining Mabel telling off the nasty Alfred Musgrave.

"In any case, I left him his whiskey and some sandwiches and whatnot, and went back to my work."

"You didn't see or hear him again?"

She frowned. "Well, about ten minutes later there was this cough, you see. I figured he was feeling poorly. The whiskey, you know. He didn't drink much usually."

Interesting. Could the cough have actually been a gunshot? One that killed Musgrave? The shot I heard had been at twenty *past* one, much later. Were there, somehow, two shots? And if what Mabel heard *was* a gun firing, then why did it sound like a cough? "What time was that? The cough, I mean."

"Musta been about one. The office is right next door, so that's prolly why I heard it. Otherwise that noise up front is too loud to hear meself think straight." She whisked the taffeta dress off the board, eyed it carefully, and hung it on the rack.

I rose from the chair. "Thank you, Mabel. That's very helpful."

"Is it?" She looked only mildly interested.

"It is," I assured her. I just wasn't sure how. As I turned to leave, she stopped me.

"Lady Rample, before you go, I think you should have this." She reached into her apron pocket and pulled out an earring. It was a flower shaped bauble of marcasite. Not expensive, but pretty.

"What's this?" I asked, taking it from her. It glittered in my hand. A vague memory nudged at the back of my mind, but I couldn't quite pull it to the forefront.

"That be Miss Josette's earring. I found it in Mrs. Fairfax's office. I was cleaning after they took the body away, and there it was. Under the desk as pretty as you please. I wasn't sure what I should do with it. Thought about giving it to the police, but you know how they are. And I didn't want to just put it back, case it were important. Figured you'd know what to do."

"Yes, thank you, Mabel." Odd that the police wouldn't have found it when they searched the room. North might be an idiot about some things, but he wasn't lazy. There was no way on God's green earth he'd have missed a sparkly earring lying next to a dead body at the time the office was examined. "Was Josette wearing these earrings the night Musgrave was killed?" I was certain she'd been wearing another pair. Green stones.

"No, m'lady. She was wearing her emeralds."

"Has anyone been in Mrs. Fairfax's office since the murder?"

"Other than Mrs. Fairfax? Caught that Coco sneaking about. Don't trust her, Milady. Not far as I can throw her. Which ain't far at all, iffen you know what I mean." She eyed my own generous curves as she let out a cackling laugh.

I grimaced. The whole modern obsession with thinness was annoying at best. "Is Coco here?"

"She's up practicing. With Josette in jail, she's gonna get the spotlight tonight."

Wouldn't she be disappointed when she discovered Josette no longer locked up. "Thank you, Mabel."

Sure enough, I found Coco Starr on the stage, crooning into the microphone. She was the antithesis of Josette. Her skin was the color of rich mahogany and her dark hair had a wide streak of white on her left side. She was a handsome woman, rather than classically beautiful, with high cheekbones and full, sultry lips. I'd put her age somewhere about forty. Her figure would have been in fashion twenty years ago, but in these days of sylph-like figures, she would kindly be called plump. But her voice... oh, her voice would make the angels weep with envy.

That deep, magnificent voice echoed through the small space, so heavy with emotion that my throat thickened and my eyes welled. She sang of sorrow and loss and love gone wrong. Of betrayal and mourning. It was all I could do to keep my composure. That British stiff upper lip. I'd never had a mere voice affect me so.

When the song came to an end, there wasn't a dry eye in the house. I noticed the pianist—not Hale, but a skinny Englishman—subtly wipe a tear from his eye.

I cleared my throat and approached the singer. "Coco Starr?"

She lifted one brow. "Yes?"

"Lady Rample." I held out my hand in the American fashion.

Coco gave me a cool look, then shook. "What can I do for you, Lady Rample?"

I held out the earring. "I'm curious about this."

Coco paused as if seriously considering her answer. Then she smiled. "Didn't fool *you*, did I?"

"Not for a bit."

She sighed. "I need a drink. Follow me." She grabbed a bottle and two glasses from behind the bar, then led me to one of the small tables for two. She sloshed a bit of amber liquid in each glass, then sipped delicately. I followed suit. Whiskey. My kind of woman. "I was trying to save Beau and the rest of the band."

I sipped my whiskey. "I'm listening." I could listen to her voice all day.

She leaned back with a sigh, looking suddenly tired. "It was always me and the boys. For five years we traveled the South with our music. Then that monster walked into our lives. Told us we would make it big in England. And we believed him. What we didn't know was that we'd basically be indentured servants to that piece of..." She shook her head and took another gulp of whiskey. "That's over now. He's gone. Don't know what we're gonna do next, but at least we're free."

"Where were you when Musgrave was killed?" I vaguely recalled Helena saying something about laryngitis. Or was that Josette? It seemed so long ago now, though it had only been a couple of days.

Coco touched her throat. "Touch of laryngitis. Doc told me to rest. Can't be damaging these pipes, you know. They're my bread and butter." She said it like butt-ah, her voice a smooth drawl. Very unlike Hale Davis's more precisely clipped tones. "I was back at the hotel, resting as ordered."

"Is there anyone who can verify that?"

"You mean give me an alibi?" Her eyes twinkled as if she found that funny. "I s'pose the hotel staff could. One of 'em brought me tea. Nasty stuff, but it did wonders."

"How far away is the hotel?"

She shrugged and tossed back a finger of whiskey before pouring herself another. "I reckon about three blocks or so."

So she had an alibi of sorts. She'd been seen at the hotel, but it was close enough she *could* have nipped out, murdered Musgrave, and got back without being seen. I wondered if North had bothered to check it out.

Probably I should do it myself. To be safe. "Why frame Josette?"

Her expression hardened. "She stole my man. Figured I'd get her back and get Beau out of jail at the same time. Stupid fool."

"So, you and Beau?"

"Married the last four years. Fell for the first pretty face come along. Idiot." From her tone, it sounded like this wasn't the first time.

"What about the note?" I asked.

"What note?"

"Telling Josette to meet backstage or you'd tell Musgrave about her and Beau."

She snorted. "I'd never do that. Musgrave would kill Beau. I wanted to get rid of Josette, not my husband. Whoever wrote that note, it wasn't me."

I believed her. So, who wrote the note luring Josette backstage? Whoever it was, it had to be the killer.

"How odd," Aunt Butty said, slathering a crumpet with copious amounts of butter before popping a bite into her mouth. "All these notes and earrings and whatnot. Bloody confusing."

"Language, Aunt Butty."

"Dash it all. I'm of an age I can swear if I bloody want to."

I grinned. Frankly, I didn't care one wit if my aunt swore a blue streak. It amused me to point it out and have her get her dander up. "Yes, it is all rather confusing."

"Perhaps we should go through the suspects one by one and see who has a motive."

"Good plan." I leaned back with my cup of tea, wishing it was a highball. This whole thing had been rather tiring.

"In murder, one always looks to the spouse, correct?"

"Sure. But Alfred Musgrave wasn't married."

"Children? Siblings?"

"None that I know of."

She sighed heavily and stuffed more crumpet in her mouth. A few crumbs fell to her ample bosom. She absently brushed them off. Today she was wearing a cherry red and white patterned silk crepe dress. Much too light for the chilly, wet weather. Not that such things ever stopped Butty from wearing exactly what she pleased. "Lovers, then."

"I believe he had two."

Her eyebrows went up. "That odious little man?"

"Life is full of surprises. Yes, Helena Fairfax, and the singer, Josette Margaux. Neither of them were happy about it."

"So, he was coercing them." Her expression hardened. "Nasty little man. Glad he's dead."

I didn't chastise her for the sentiment. I rather shared it. If anyone deserved bumping off, it was Alfred Musgrave. "Let's start with Helena Fairfax. They owned the club together, and I understand he was trying to force her out. Not to mention he was cheating on her."

"If he *was* coercing her, she should have been relieved," Aunt Butty pointed out.

"True." Which was what made her supposed jealousy over Musgrave so unlikely. "There was also the threat he'd tell her husband."

"She stood to lose her livelihood, her family, and her reputation. All excellent motives for murder," Butty said decisively around a mouthful of buttered crumpet. "What about this singer? Josette?"

"She was in love with the saxophonist, Beauford Parks. Who, by the by, is married to the other singer, Coco Starr."

"Now there's a fine kettle of fish. What's Josette's motive?"

"She was afraid Alfred would discover her affair with Beau and kill him. Or both of them. Which, from what I know of Musgrave, isn't that far-fetched. Plus, Musgrave had been forcing himself on her for some time. Good motive for murder there."

Aunt Butty nodded. "Good motive for Beau, too." She selected a pink-frosted petite four from the tray and eyed it closely before taking a bite of it.

"Sure," I agreed. "Except Josette and Beau both have alibis."

"What about this Coco person?"

"Coco Starr. Stunning voice. She had plenty of motive to kill her husband or Josette, not much to kill Musgrave, although she clearly didn't like him and was worried about what he'd do to Beau. I need to double check her alibi, but I'm not convinced she did it."

"I suppose it's the same for the rest of the band," Butty muttered as she selected another petite four.

"Unfortunately, yes. Not much motive other than vague dislike."

She held up one finger. "But Mr. Fairfax had an excellent motive. Musgrave was diddling his wife!"

I winced at her choice of words. "Rather. However, I met the man. Let's just say his faculties are rather impaired by his penchant for opium."

She dropped another lump of sugar in her tea and stirred vigorously. "Which doesn't let him off the hook."

"True," I agreed. "He could have found out about Musgrave and Helena and killed the man in a drug induced jealous rage, but he doesn't seem the type. Still, I suppose I should keep him on the list."

"Anyone else?"

I remembered a mousy man with glasses. "John Bamber."

"Who the blazes is he?"

"The club manager. He looked very nervous when he overheard Musgrave and Helena talking about the audit. What if there was something fishy in the books? Helena all but admitted she'd been skimming. Surely she would have needed help with that."

"That wouldn't look good for Bamber. And if Musgrave took over the entire club, he'd fire Bamber for sure," Aunt Butty said. "Possibly have him thrown in prison."

"Exactly."

She sighed, leaning back with her teacup clutched to her bosom. "Four strong suspects, if you count Helena. All with very good motives. How are we going to figure out the real killer?"

That was the question. One for which, currently, I had no answer.

Shéa MacLeod

Chapter 13

The hotel where Coco and the rest of the musicians had been staying was precisely three and a half blocks from the Astoria Club. It was an easy walk which had taken less than five minutes. Easy enough for Coco to get to the club, kill Musgrave, and get back without anyone noticing she'd been gone.

The place looked more like a flop house than a proper hotel, complete with a faded sign over the door which read "Valmont Hotel: Rooms to Let." The narrow brick building was crammed tight between the Cambridge Pub and a coffee shop popular with the artistic set. Across the street, the elegant turrets of the Palace Theatre in all its elegant Victorian glory rose against the leaden sky. I sighed. Looked like rain again.

As far as I could see, the only way out of the hotel was through the front door. And while there was no doorman—shocking, I know—a chubby young man with a wispy, blond attempt at a moustache perched behind the registration desk just inside the door. Glad I'd worn my chocolate brown gauntlet gloves—elegant and would hide any dirt I might pick up—I pushed open the door. The place did not look clean. The carpet was an eye-searing array of cabbage roses in greens and reds, faded and thread-worn. The faint smell of cabbage permeated the air.

"Pardon me." I used my most Lady Rample of tones. As if I were the Queen herself coming to visit.

The boy—for he was hardly more than that—glanced up from his magazine. "Oh! Oh, Milady." He was instantly flushed and flustered. "What can I… What are you… This ain't no place…"

I slapped down a pound note with a slightly flirtatious smile. "You *are* aware of the musicians from America staying at this establishment."

He looked blank for a moment, as if I'd spoken in Mandarin or some such. "Americans? Yes. Yes. They got two rooms between 'em."

"The woman. Coco Starr. You've seen her, of course."

He nodded. "Yes, madam. I mean, Milady."

"Do you recall a few nights ago when she was ill?"

"'Course, Milady. Had me runnin' around gettin' her soup and whatnot." He gave a grimace. "Had to work the night shift that day of all days."

"Did you ever see her leave the hotel?"

"No, Milady. She never even left her room. Not since I come on at eight."

I leaned closer, nudging the note toward him. "You're absolutely certain?"

"Yes, Milady. Positive. Like I said, had me runnin' to her room every five minutes with tea and soup and lord knows. Ooops." He flushed. "Sorry, Milady."

I waved him off. "And you're certain that she couldn't have slipped out while you were getting the soup or tea? Say around midnight?"

"Oh, no, Milady. See, at night we keep the doors locked for safety at ten. Whoever is on duty has to let people in or out. Ain't nobody could have got out 'less I let 'em out."

"Thank you." I slipped him the note and stepped back outside as quickly as I could without being too obvious. Relieved to be in the fresh air once more, I quickly took stock.

While time-wise Coco was in the running for murdering Musgrave, the fact that the hotel was locked three hours before the murder took place made it impossible for her to have done so. I mentally crossed her off the list. One down. Too bad the rest wouldn't be as easy.

Another dull party I couldn't get out of. The same dull people as always. Unfortunately, Lord Dalton kept his study—and therefore his whiskey—locked up tight. Chaz had disappeared somewhere, so I couldn't make use of his lock picking skills. I was, alas, reduced to drinking sherry.

Eventually I made my way to the terrace and from there into the garden. Soft laughter echoed from the bushes as couples disappeared into the dark for assignations of one nature or the other.

At the very back of the garden was an empty bench, half hidden from view beneath an overgrown wisteria. I sank onto it, grateful for a moment of quiet. In the darkness, the tip of a cigarette flared orange.

"Who's there?" I demanded.

A shadow moved in the dark. In the faint light spilling from the house, I could just make out his features as Hale Davis moved into the light.

"What are you doing here? Shouldn't you be at the club?"

"It's early yet." His voice was a low rumble, smooth as velvet and sexy as sin.

"That doesn't answer the question. What are you doing *here*?"

"Lord of the Manor liked how I play. Hired me for a couple sets. Figured I'd squeeze in a smoke before the second."

"I don't think you're supposed to be back here."

He shrugged. "Too bad. Not in the habit of doing what I'm supposed to do."

I suppressed a grin. "Cheeky. I like it."

He gave me a look I couldn't quite interpret, but the smolder in his gaze never dampened. "You're the lady detective."

I laughed. "Don't let Detective Inspector North hear you say that. I'm not exactly what he considers detective material."

"Oh?"

"Wrong body parts."

He grinned. "Guess you're not in the habit of doing what you're supposed to, either."

"Not in the least." I leaned back on the bench, crossing one leg over the other in a decidedly un-ladylike fashion. "I don't know your name." Total lie, of course, but I didn't want *him* to know I'd been asking about him.

"I don't know yours." We stared at each other for a few heartbeats. The air between us was thick enough to choke on. "Hale Davis." He held out his hand.

His hand engulfed mine, warm and firm, smooth except for slightly rough calluses on his fingers from playing. In the darkness, my skin was moonglow bright against his. Something zinged up my spine. We held hands a little longer than strictly necessary. "Ophelia Rample."

"Don't you mean *Lady* Rample?" he asked, letting go of my hand at last.

"If you care about that sort of thing."

He sat down without asking. He smelled faintly of cigarette smoke, and beneath that, something citrusy. "Do *you* care about that sort of thing?"

"When you're richer than God, you don't *have* to care about that sort of thing. People will forgive you for all sorts of nonsense."

He lifted a brow. "Including not knowing your place?"

I didn't smile, because I knew he wasn't talking about the difference in our genders or stations. The world was an ugly place sometimes. "I suppose it depends."

"That's what I thought." He tossed his cigarette to the ground, grinding it out with his foot. "Find the killer yet?" he asked, changing the subject.

"Not yet." It didn't escape me that I might be sitting next to the murderer. After all, I knew nothing of this man. What if he'd had a reason to shoot Alfred Musgrave? Except that was ridiculous. He'd been onstage playing the piano when Musgrave was shot. I couldn't think of a better alibi than that. Even if he wanted to kill Musgrave, he couldn't possibly have done it. "What will you do now Musgrave is dead? Will you stay in London? Or go back to the States?"

"The coppers won't let us leave the country. Fortunately, Mrs. Fairfax has asked us to stay on, keep playing. Works for me." He stared into the dark. "After that, who knows."

We sat in silence for a moment. It wasn't uncomfortable, but it was full of things unspoken. Finally, I had to ask. "How did you feel about Alfred Musgrave?"

He sneered. "Now that's something I can't repeat to a lady."

"So you didn't care for him."

"Putting it mildly."

That wasn't good. "What did he do?"

"What *didn't* he do? Man was a racist, sexist slime. When he wasn't molesting the women, he was threatening the men, docking our pay, ordering us about like we were on a plantation."

I shuddered. I'd read about that. The horrific things done to people. It was shocking and horrifying to me. "Did you kill him?"

He smiled and there was something deadly in it. "No. If I'd have killed him, it wouldn't have been cowardly with a gun to the back of the head. I would have met him face to face like a man. Beat him to death with my own fists."

His words chilled me, but they also made sense. I didn't know this man, but his character was clear to me. He was the sort to face a problem head on. Killing from behind wasn't his style. That he could kill at all was somewhat shocking, but then again, I suppose any of us could kill given the right impetus.

I cleared my throat. "Tell me about your life in America."

He gave me a long look. "I've got to get back. Job to do. Why don't we have a drink later, and I'll tell you all about it." There was a husky quality to his tone, promising more than a mere drink. "Meet me at the club tonight."

"All right," I found myself saying.

With that, he melted into the shadows. I stayed in the darkness for a while, as piano music drifted toward me on the evening breeze.

I had hoped to convince Chaz to accompany me to the Astoria Club again, but alas, he was otherwise occupied, having found a French Count with scintillating stories of his world travels. I was fairly certain Chaz was less interested in the stories than the count himself. I had no issue leaving him to his devices, but it left me in a quandary.

As often as I enjoyed throwing convention to the wind, a single lady at a jazz club would have stirred scandal of epic proportions. Asking Varant to accompany me to meet another man simply wasn't on, and Aunt Butty—for all her bohemian wildness—couldn't stand jazz. Although she didn't go so far as to call it the Devil's music, as my father no doubt would, she shuddered every time I brought it up.

There was only one thing for it. The club closed at three. At a quarter to, I drove my Roadster into Soho and parked a block from the club. As I watched the door, I wished for the first time I smoked. It would have given me a way to occupy my time instead of fidgeting like a teenager at a country dance.

I carefully considered my reaction to Hale Davis. Frankly, it was ridiculous. I was a grown woman who didn't get flustered over handsome men. Especially not handsome inappropriate men. And Hale Davis was the epitome of inappropriate. He was a *musician,* for God's sake. Imagining the stir it would cause in the upper echelons of society was enough to make the strongest quail. Not that such a thing would stop me were it true love.

I laughed at my own nonsense. True love? I'd only just met the man. Right now, it was a simple case of lust.

Varant, on the other hand, was imminently suitable. Handsome, yes. Rich, *my* yes. And a Lord, to boot. His family was of the very best. Yes, he'd be suitable. And he was surprisingly progressive and supportive of my desire to play detective, but I worried he'd also be dull. And while there was a certain chemistry between us now, I feared that eventually I would be forced into the part of Lady Varant with a fake smile plastered to my face and ice shards in my heart.

No, staying a merry widow had more perks than draw backs. Aunt Butty had certainly proven that. Lord Rample's name gave me a shield more precious than the mounds of gold he'd left me. I shook my head, amused by my own thoughts.

The door to the club swung open and patrons, half-drunk with music and booze, stumbled out laughing and calling to each other. A man grabbed a young woman and pulled her into a shadowy doorway, kissing her thoroughly. She kissed him back with abandon. Then they ran into the night, giggling like school children.

Eventually the stream of humanity stopped. And then the door opened again, and out came the musicians smoking cigarettes and slouching with fatigue. I immediately made out Hale Davis, straight and tall at the back, his handsome features highlighted by the street lamps. I knew the minute he saw me even though his expression didn't change.

Faintly I heard him bid the others goodnight as they turned and walked away down the pavement just as the clouds opened up and rain poured down. Up went black umbrellas and the rest of them scurried into the night.

Hale pulled up his collar, ducked his head, and dashed to my car, sliding into the passenger's seat. "Lady Rample." His eyes were inscrutable in the dim light.

"Mr. Davis."

He grinned, his teeth a slash of white. "How clandestine."

"I do love a secret assignation." Was that my voice all breathy?

His grin widened. "There's a bar not far from here. We can walk."

I eyed the rain still pouring down, forming puddles on the pavement. "How far?"

"Two blocks."

"All right." I grabbed my brolly from the back seat. "Lead on."

Huddled beneath my umbrella, we scurried down the sidewalk. Our breaths mingled in the chill air.

"This way." He guided me into an alleyway. I had a moment of suspicion until he knocked on a black, unmarked door. It cracked open and an eyeball appeared. Then the door swung fully open and Hale ushered me inside.

It turned out to be, quite literally, an underground club, serving alcohol long past what the law allowed. Likely it was the closest thing to an American speakeasy in London.

A narrow staircase led down into a large room with bare floorboards, pressed tin ceilings, and rickety tables and chairs scattered about. The bar was well stocked and the patrons bohemian. This place did not cater to the upper crust, but to the artists, musicians, writers, and leftists of London. It was not the sort of place a lady should be seen in, and I loved it immediately.

We sat at the bar, also something a lady should never do, and ordered drinks. A highball for me and straight-up whiskey for him. There was no ice, so my drink was warm, the ginger ale was unusually spicy, and the whiskey sharp and cheap. Still, I didn't mind. I was too busy drinking in the atmosphere and the energy radiating from the man sitting next to me.

In my world, a black man and white woman sitting together would have caused raised eyebrows and polite outrage. Here, no one noticed. No one cared. In fact, we were far from the only interracial couple in the place. It made sense. There were more women than men in Britain since The War, and rejecting love on the basis of skin color seemed... utterly ridiculous. I knew Aunt Butty agreed with me. Her second husband had been born in India of a British father and Sikh mother. It had caused quite a stir back in the day. Possibly it was why she'd hired Mr. Singh as her butler.

We talked of inane things at first, and then I asked, "Where are you from?"

"I was born in New York, but music has taken me all over. Especially after I joined up with Beau and Coco. They're from New Orleans."

"Did you live there? New Orleans?" It had always seemed a fascinating place to me. Romantic. Perhaps one day I'd visit.

"For a time. Every jazz musician worth his salt hits New Orleans at one time or another. I just happened to hit and stay awhile."

"How long awhile?"

He grinned. "Ten years."

"How long have Beau and Coco been together?"

He lifted a brow as if to let me know he knew what I was doing. "Since they were hardly more than kids. They've been married four years now."

"And how many times has he cheated on her?"

He shook his head. "Don't miss much, do you?"

I didn't say anything, simply watched as he toyed with his glass with those long, elegant fingers. I tried very hard not to imagine those fingers playing over my skin.

"I guess from the beginning. Volatile, that's what they call it. They're all heat and fire and passion. But it burns hot and fast, you know? And then they can't stand the sight of each other. He goes off, finds himself someone willing. Coco finds out, gets all het up, gives him a tongue-lashing. They make up and start all over again."

"Sounds exhausting."

He grinned. "Maybe. But it seems to work for them. And don't believe Coco is an innocent. She's had her share of men on the side. Women, too."

That surprised me. "Really?"

"If rumor is to be believed, she and Josette were an item before Beau got to her."

By golly, if that didn't take the cake. That was one thing I didn't see coming. Could it be that Josette and Coco were somehow in on the murder together? Might Coco have been jealous of Musgrave? Or angry that he was forcing himself on her former lover? Or maybe Josette had Coco wrapped around her little finger. Convinced her that Musgrave needed to die. Was Coco really in her hotel when Musgrave was killed? I didn't see how she could have been anywhere else, but one never knew.

"I can see the wheels turning." Hale's voice interrupted my musings. "Penny for your thoughts."

I wasn't sure if I should let him in on my new theory. It was a wild shot in the dark, after all, and probably didn't amount to anything. Still, he could have some valuable insight. "I was wondering if Coco and Josette could have been in on the murder together."

That made him laugh. "I can't imagine those two committing murder. Either of them. And certainly not together. Any tender feelings they may have had are long gone. They hate each other with the heat of a thousand suns."

"Why? If Coco is used to Beau cheating on her, why would she be more upset than usual?"

"I think it's the first time she truly believes someone could steal him permanently."

"Oh." Well, that didn't sound good. I felt bad for Coco. "Do you have any, ah, family?"

He gave me a knowing look. "Ain't married, if that's what you're asking. No woman, either. Not for a long time."

I shifted, feeling suddenly warm. "Children?" I blurted. After all, plenty of men had children without being married to their mothers.

"Not that I know of. What about you?" He leaned a little closer. "What's your story? How'd you end up in London?"

"What makes you think I'm not *from* here?" I took a sip of my drink, pretending his nearness didn't make my heart flutter.

"You're different from all them other… what's the term? Toffs." He grinned. Rather cheekily, too.

"I'm from the Cotswolds," I admitted. "But my aunt came and rescued me when I was sixteen. Brought me to London."

"Rescued you. That sounds like a story."

And not a story I was ready to tell a virtual stranger. Fortunately, the two-man band started playing something dance-worthy and Hale grabbed my hand. "Come."

Several other couples hit the dance floor at once, and Hale swept me around the outer edges and into the center. I was used to dancing with Chaz. Dancing with Hale was a whole new experience. Where Chaz was all elegance and grace, tightly restrained, perfectly balanced, Hale's moves were smoother, wilder. There was more energy and movement. He never lost a step or missed a beat, but he threw in an extra flourish here and there, just out of pure fun.

Something built between us. Something that set off a fire low in my belly and brought a flush to my cheeks. The musky scent of him, the sweat glistening on his brow. My breath came short and fast and it had nothing to do with the dance and everything to do with the man.

At last the song ended and Hale led me from the floor back to the bar. I was both relieved and disappointed. I probably downed my drink a little too fast. But it was either that or make a fool of myself. I pressed my palm against the coolness of the wooden bar, willing myself to maintain decorum.

Hale traced a finger across the back of my hand. His voice was a low rumble in my ear. "Listen, Ophelia—"

A disturbance at the door drew our attention. A newcomer staggered into the club, drunk as a lord. A few of the rougher customers greeted him, which surprised me. He was well-dressed and clearly of a better class of person, if one discounted his current state. I recognized him instantly as Helena's husband, Leo Fairfax. The man was everywhere these days.

"Damn, what's he doing here?" Hale muttered, withdrawing his hand from mine. Again, that strange mix of relief and disappointment.

"Good question." I turned to stare again. It was definitely the man Chaz and I had run into outside The Astoria Club. I noticed one of the men at a nearby table slip Leo Fairfax a roll of pound notes. In return, Leo handed him something, though I couldn't tell what. Whatever it was, it was small enough to fit in the man's palm.

Hale swore under his breath and grabbed my arm. "We should get out of here."

"What's going on?"

"Don't look. Pretend you didn't notice anything. I'll explain when we get outside." He slapped some bills on the bar, then hustled me up the stairs and outside without a backward glance.

As we left the club, the rain had stopped, and the sun painted the morning horizon pink and orange. It would have been romantic if I wasn't so focused on what had just happened. I stopped in the middle of the pavement, refusing to budge another inch. "Now explain."

Hale's expression was grim as he took my arm and pulled me gently toward the tiny park across the street known as Golden Square. This early in the morning it was empty, the statue of King George II standing quiet sentinel to the dawn.

"It's not common knowledge," Hale said as we walked, "but Leo has been in the opium game for quite some time."

"Yes, I know."

That surprised him. "You do?"

"A—ah—friend of mine used be involved in that world years ago. He knew Leo back in the day. Was that what was happening? Leo was selling opium?"

Hale nodded. "Mostly he deals it out of his wife's club, but occasionally he sells elsewhere. Wherever he can make a buck."

I assumed "buck" meant "pound," or "dollar," I suppose, since he was American. This confirmed what Aunt Butty had told me about Leo Fairfax and his drugs problem. "Leo's selling drugs in the Astoria Club?" I asked, surprised Helena would let him get away with it. I'd have bashed the blighter over the head. Felix had not approved of drugs, nor did I. Even Aunt Butty, for all her Bohemian ways, would not tolerate anything stronger than cannabis.

"Yeah. But Musgrave found out and threatened to turn him in. Guess Leo's expanded his trade." He didn't sound like he cared one way or the other about it.

Perhaps the Astoria Club wasn't the best place for Chaz to be spending time. Not if it was the center of Leo's opium trade. Chaz didn't need the temptation. Perhaps I should speak to him about it.

"Why didn't you want to tell me inside?"

He grimaced. "Never know who's listening. Don't want it getting in the wrong ears, ya know?"

I didn't, but I let it go. The drugs world was not my cup of tea, as it were. "Could Leo Fairfax have killed Alfred Musgrave?" I asked as he led me over to a bench where we took a seat. The stone seat was rather chilly on my nether regions and I shivered.

Hale draped an arm around my shoulders. "Doubt it. He's too busy hitting the pipe."

I wasn't familiar with the term, but imagined it had something to do with taking opium. Still, getting kicked out of his wife's club for dealing drugs was a good reason for wanting Musgrave dead. I wasn't about to write Leo off my suspect list. Not just yet.

I hesitated, unsure of what to say next. An unusual occurrence for me. But then, Hale Davis was unlike any man I'd ever met. His arm was a warm contrast to the nip of the morning air. The musky, citrus scent of him stirred me in ways I hadn't been since... oh, ever. The heat I'd felt in the no-name club returned. Aunt Butty would have approved. Myself, I found it equal parts disturbing and thrilling. I was used to men being interested in me. I wasn't used to returning the favor. I found I enjoyed my freedom.

"I should be getting home," Hale said finally.

I cleared my throat. "Give you a lift to your hotel?"

Hale refused the ride. "I'm only a couple blocks away. I could use the walk." He didn't move. If anything, he drew me a little closer. The heat of him pressed all along my side and I felt suddenly giddy.

"If you're sure." My stomach fluttered strangely.

He gave me a look that sent heat surging into body parts long quiet. Then he took me in his arms and kissed me thoroughly right there in the park in front of God and anyone who might be awake at that ghastly hour.

His lips were soft and supple. His breath mingled intimately with mine. His tongue, oh his tongue was erotic velvet. Just when I was about to do something thoroughly unladylike—like melt into a puddle or hike up my gown and straddle him—he jumped up, bid me goodnight, and strode down the street without a backward glance.

Feeling a little flustered, I watched him go, unsure how to react. Somewhere in the back of my mind I realized my lipstick no doubt needed refreshing. It wouldn't do to get caught mussed up. I opened my evening bag to retrieve the tube, and a small, white feather fluttered to my lap. I picked it up and eyed it carefully. Something in the back of my muddled mind stirred.

A gunshot that sounded like a cough.
A single feather on the floor.
No pillows in Helena's office.
I needed to visit the club right away!

Chapter 14

The next day, I found myself in front of the Astoria Club again. The place was starting to feel like a second home. I was spending a ridiculous amount of time here.

I'd barely slept, eager to discover if I was right. But I'd been forced to wait until a reasonable hour to put my plan into action.

Helena was sitting at her desk, back to the door, riffling through paperwork as if nothing had happened. Apparently, the police had released her office. I wasn't sure I could sit quite so calmly in a dead man's chair.

I glanced around. No pillows.

I cleared my throat and she whirled around, hand to heart. "Oh, Lady Rample. You startled me."

"Ophelia," I reminded her. "North let you back in, I see." I took a seat, uninvited. The plush, pink armchair looked too inviting. I was trying to think of a way to bring up the pillow situation. I'd seen her using one in her temporary office, but the room was devoid of anything so frivolous.

"Yes. They've taken all the fingerprints and whatnot they needed. Good thing, too. The work is piling up, as you can see." She held out one pale, delicate hand to indicate the mound of papers and files on her desk. "I can't afford to stay closed, regardless of the situation."

"I had no idea there was so much paperwork involved in running a club," I said, leaning back. It was awkward, as if the seat was a bit too deep. I shifted uneasily. There really should be a pillow. Just a small one for the lower back. I had a chair just like it at home and it had a pillow. A thought wriggled its way into my mind. I had to ask. "I don't suppose you have a pillow anywhere? This seat is dashed uncomfortable without it."

A faint frown line appeared between her eyes. "There was one…" She glanced about vaguely. "I've no idea what happened to it…"

"No matter." I brushed it aside, careful not to reveal my true intentions. "You were saying? About the paperwork?"

"I decided to finish the audit." Helena patted one of the large piles.

That was interesting. Why would she finish the audit if she was the one skimming? To better hide her thievery? But why, if Musgrave was gone? She didn't need to hide anything. As full owner, she could take whatever she chose out of the kitty, as long as she was honest about it with the tax man.

"I did skim, as you deduced," she explained. I was surprised by her bald admission. "But not as much as Alfred claimed. I kept careful records. Just in case." She handed me a small, gold-foil covered notebook.

Inside, in small, dainty script, were columns of numbers. Dates and amounts, from the looks of things. I did a few quick calculations in my head. I'd always been rather good at math.

"Looks like about two hundred pounds over the past several months." That was, perhaps, a couple of months' wages taken over quite some time. Not enough to really raise eyebrows.

"Exactly. Money is tight. I needed a little extra to cover household expenses." Her grim expression told me her household expenses had a lot to do with her husband. "But Alfred claimed closer to two thousand pounds was missing within the last six months. I never took that much, as you can see."

"Yes. I can see that." If her little book was accurate. But I could see no reason why she'd keep a fake book of embezzlement. It was dashed odd. "Who else would have the means and opportunity to take this money?" I asked as I handed back the book.

"Alfred, of course. And since he's the one who wanted the audit, I can only assume it wasn't him."

"I agree. What about your husband?"

"I don't let him near the money or the books," she said dryly. "For good reason."

From her expression, I assumed she knew—or at least assumed—I was aware of her husband's penchant for opium. "What about what's his name? The manager?"

"John Bamber? Well, yes, of course he has access to the books. Plus, he makes the deposits most mornings. In fact," she lowered her voice, "he's the one who was helping me out. I believe it's what is referred to as 'cooking the books.' He assured me Alfred would never know."

"Apparently, he got that wrong." And if Alfred found out, it would be a very good motive for murder. "Is he here now? Mr. Bamber?"

"I believe he's at the bar. We're expecting a shipment of liquor today."

"Then let's go have a chat with him." I had started to rise when Mabel staggered through the open doorway, face white as a sheet.

"Mrs. Fairfax!"

"What is it, Mabel?" Her tone was one of exasperation. "Can't you see I'm busy?"

"Sorry, Missus, but it's Mr. Bamber. He done tried to kill himself!"

"What?" Helena rose from her chair, mouth and eyes wide.

"Come see for yourself, ma'am!" Mabel beckoned wildly and took off down the hall.

I charged after her with Helena close on my heels. I was glad I'd worn my wide legged trousers and low-heeled t-straps. All this dashing about was bloody exhausting.

In the dressing room, stretched out on the fainting couch with a pillow beneath his head, we found John Bamber. He was unconscious, breathing shallow and skin white as milk. On a low table beside him was a glass of water and several empty papers that had likely contained sleeping powders. Next to that was a neatly printed note on a scrap of torn paper. I picked it up. It said simply:

I CAN'T GO ON.

How very melodramatic.

Helena went to her knees beside him. "John! John! Wake up." She gave him a little shake, but there was no response.

There was nothing for it. I reached down and slapped him hard enough to leave a pink mark on his cheek. He gave a moan, but nothing else. "Mabel, call the doctor immediately. And then bring us a glass of milk."

"Yes, m'lady." She scurried off to do my bidding.

"Why are you thinking of milk at a time like this?" Helena wailed.

My, the melodrama was catching. "Because, you idiot, that's what you're supposed to drink after you've poisoned yourself. It lines the stomach so the poison doesn't penetrate."

Her eyes widened. "How did you know that?"

"I trained as a nurse during the War." Not to mention I read a lot. I certainly had as a girl. And I'd been fascinated by morbid things such as poisons and murder. I was currently a huge fan of the Queen of Mystery, Agatha Christie. I'd read all her works and eagerly awaited the next. Of course, finding a poisoning victim in real life wasn't nearly so exciting.

Mabel returned, glass of milk sloshing in her hand. "They're on their way." She shoved the glass at me.

"Thank you. Now, let's get him up so I can get this down his throat."

Between the three of us, we managed to hoist him into a sitting position, and I forced the milk down his throat. I think we got more on the couch than we did in him, but I hoped it was enough.

Fortunately, Dr. Eliot arrived with his nurse and shooed us away. Once the ghastly noises started, Helena and I hurried to the bar, well out of earshot.

"Drink?" she asked, rounding the bar and eyeballing the bottles of liquor.

"Don't mind if I do. Highball, please."

She smiled. "Good choice."

After pouring whiskey, ginger ale, and ice into a glass for me, she made herself a Sidecar. We sat at the bar, side by side, nursing our drinks.

"He tried to kill himself, didn't he?" Helena said finally.

"Looks that way." Though something niggled in my mind. Something not quite right.

"Why do you suppose he did it?"

I twisted my glass, watching the amber liquid swirl inside. "I imagine he was afraid Musgrave would catch him at it."

"But Alfred is dead."

"True. But you decided to go ahead with the audit. Up until now, you've believed his only wrong doing was to help you hide a bit of money. He knew the minute you finished the audit, you'd know the truth. He was using your skimming to hide his own. And he was stealing a lot more."

She shook her head. "He should have come to me. He should have told me. I'd have helped him. Why would he do that?"

I shrugged and took a sip of my drink. She would have made a damn fine barman. "Who knows? Maybe he was in a spot of trouble and didn't realize you'd help him. Maybe he thought he could pay it back before anyone knew it was gone. Maybe he enjoyed the thrill. I've read some do."

"He was such a kind man," she said morosely. "Always willing to help a girl out when she needed it. I guess we'll never know why he did it."

I gave her a startled look which she didn't see. "He's not dead yet. The doctor may have gotten to him in time."

There was the merest pause. "Oh, yes. Let's hope so."

Again, I eyed her, but she appeared sincere. "Yes, let's."

"Maybe he's the one who killed Alfred," she said after a bit.

"What do you mean?"

"Perhaps it's like you said. Poor John believed Alfred was going to catch him out, so he killed Alfred. Then guilt got the better of him. That's John for you. Very sensitive. He would definitely feel guilty about being forced to murder someone." She smiled widely as if she'd solved the crime single handedly.

"It's a good hypothesis." If a bit obvious.

"We should tell the police." She took a sip of her Sidecar, made a face, and added a healthy dose of cognac.

I repressed a shudder. Cognac was possibly my least favorite beverage. "Of course. I'll mention it to DI North." Maybe.

Helena had made an excellent point. It made sense, this motive for Alfred's murder and John Bamber's attempt at suicide, but something felt off. Something didn't quite ring true. I just couldn't figure out what it was.

Detective Inspector North arrived a few minutes after Dr. Eliot. After a brief confab with the doctor, North took over Helena's office for questioning. Mabel was the first one in, as she was the one who found Bamber unconscious.

Being of the nosy variety, I left Helena to a second cocktail, slipped past the uniformed policeman North had posted outside Helena's office, and into the dressing room where we'd found Bamber. Apparently North considered the event an attempted suicide and therefore didn't post a guard on the dressing room itself. The pillow had fallen off the chaise longue and onto the floor. I picked it up and examined it carefully. It was perfectly intact. A search of the rest of the room revealed two more pillows, all intact. I swore silently.

I slipped back down the hall and took up a position where I could overhear. I was well aware from previous visits that voices could be heard from within the ladies' WC. So I told the guard I needed to use the necessary—which made him blush like a tomato—and locked myself in the tiny room. Taking my empty Highball glass out of my handbag, I pressed it to the wall and listened carefully. The voices were slightly distorted, but the words were clear enough.

"—I never was so shocked in all my days!" It was Mabel at her most dramatic. "He was just lying there like the dead. I near passed out."

"But you didn't." Even with the distortion, North's voice was dry as dust.

"'Course not." She sounded offended he'd had the temerity to ask such a thing. "I went and got the ladies."

"By which you mean Lady Rample and Mrs. Fairfax?"

"'Course. Who else?" Her tone indicated she considered him an idiot of the first order.

"Did you touch anything in the room? Anything at all?"

"Not a thing. Just saw him and ran. Figured what with the note and all, he done somethin' stupid."

North cleared his throat. "Did you see anyone else here?"

"Only some'at earlier. The musician wot plays that saxophone. Devil's music, you ask me."

I almost dropped the glass, I was that surprised. Beau Parks had been here? I hadn't seen him.

"Do you mean Beauford Parks?" North asked with surprising patience.

"That's the one," Mabel affirmed.

"Was he anywhere near John Bamber?"

"'Course. They was arguing fit to burst. Quiet like, though. Hissin' like snakes."

"What time was this?" North asked.

Mabel made a humming sound as if trying to dredge up a faded memory. "Oh, 'least half hour before I found Bamber out cold."

Which would give Beau plenty of time to poison Bamber. If he had been poisoned.

"Could you hear what they said during the argument?" North asked.

"Not a word."

"Thank you, Mabel. That is all."

I heard the door to the office open and North muttering with the officer on duty. I quickly tucked the glass behind the waste basket. No need to get caught in the act, so to speak. With a quick check in the mirror to see all was in order, I unlocked the door and stepped into the hall.

"Ah, Lady Rample. Just the woman."

I gave North a bland smile. "Detective Inspector."

"Please." He gestured toward the open door. "Join me. I have some questions."

"But of course." I strode in and took a seat, eyeing him calmly as if I hadn't a care in the world. But my mind was reeling. Why was Beau arguing with John Bamber? Why was he *here*? Could I have been wrong? Could Beau be behind all this, after all? And if so, what did that mean for Coco? And Josette? Could they have faked their alibis? It seemed impossible.

North sat down heavily. There were dark bags beneath his eyes and his suit was rumpled. I caught a whiff of stale cigarettes and old tea. Not entirely pleasant.

"What are you doing here, Lady Rample?" His voice sounded as tired as he looked.

"Just visiting a friend, Detective Inspector. No crime in that, is there?"

He rubbed his forehead. "I'm beginning to think everything you do is a crime."

I wasn't sure whether to be pleased or offended, so I ignored the comment. "Did you know Helena plans to carry out the audit Musgrave had been doing when he was killed?"

"Interesting." Neither his tone nor his expression gave away any emotion. The man was frustrating.

"She and I both believe Bamber was cooking the books. You know, skimming money."

"I do know what 'cooking the books' means, Lady Rample. And I know all about it. That's probably why Bamber tried to kill himself."

"Tried? Then he's going to live?"

He rubbed his forehead again. "The doc thinks he'll live."

"That's a relief. He seemed a nice man, if rather sad. By the way, you do know that he didn't try to kill himself, don't you?"

He let out a strangled sound which may have been one of frustration. "Do tell."

"Well, you see, it's like this. The scene was too perfect."

He rolled his eyes. "Is that it?"

"No, of course not." Honestly, if the man would just let me speak! "John Bamber was exactly the sort of man who would kill himself in exactly the sort of spot of bother that would force his hand."

"I don't follow."

I tapped my fingers on the edge of the armchair. "Let me put it like this. Imagine you want to kill someone because—oh, I don't know—they know something you don't want getting out. Something that could send you to prison. Or worse. What do you do? If you're of the criminal persuasion, that is."

He picked up an empty teacup and stared inside morosely as if willing more tea to magically appear. "I suppose I'd threaten him."

"But threatening someone can't be assured. Not if something scarier comes along."

"True," North admitted. "I suppose—if I were of the criminal persuasion as you so succinctly put it—I would have to kill him."

"Exactly," I agreed. "But you wouldn't want to raise suspicion, correct? So how would you go about getting rid of such a man?"

North leaned back, crossing his ankles and eyeing me not unlike a snake eyes a tasty rabbit. "I would find his weakness. The thing that would make him easy to kill."

"Naturally. Take an alcoholic. It would be easy enough to kill him with drink or the result of drink. For instance, a fall into a canal. Oh, dear. He's drowned. I told him walking home drunk was dangerous! You see? Easy enough *and* a murder is masked as an accident."

His eyes glittered. "Are you telling me you believe someone tried to take advantage of Bamber's depressed nature to get rid of him through a fake suicide?"

"That's exactly what I'm saying, Detective Inspector."

He pondered that. "What's your proof?"

"I haven't any," I admitted. "Except for one thing. The suicide note."

"What of it?"

"It was written on a scrap of paper. Why would a person who was about to commit suicide write his last declaration on a bit of rubbish?"

"That's still not proof," North pointed out.

"Of course not," I admitted. "But if I were you, I'd guard Bamber very closely until he's able to tell you what he knows that would make someone want to kill him."

"I'll take that under advisement, Lady Rample."

"See that you do." I stood to leave, but then remembered the entire reason I'd come there in the first place. "By the way, when you were first inspecting the scene of Alfred Musgrave's death, I don't suppose you or your men found any pillows with holes in them?"

"Er, no. We found some feathers in one of the dustbins and several intact pillows in the dressing room, but none with holes. Why do you ask?"

"No reason," I said, brightly. "Toodles, Detective." And I sailed from the room. Feathers in the dust bin. How interesting.

Chapter 15

"What a fine kettle of fish," Aunt Butty said with a slight shake of her head. The wax grapes clustered on the side of her hat trembled dangerously. The urge to reach out and grab them before they tumbled to the floor was almost irresistible.

She had popped 'round ostensibly for luncheon, but it was clear it was gossip she was after.

"Indeed. I simply don't know what to do next." I didn't bother to explain that it wasn't only the murder—and the attempted murder—that stumped me. There were two men in my life who were causing a great deal of consternation.

"What about this Bamber fellow? Has that copper figured out yet what he knows?"

"Unfortunately, the last I heard, Bamber was still unconscious." Not that North would tell me anything anyway. I'd have to beg Varant to hit him up for information. It was my only option, though I worried it would send Varant the wrong message. Or perhaps the right message. Really, it was most baffling.

"What do we do now?" Butty asked.

Her excitement surprised me. "I'm not sure. I'm at a bit of a loss."

"Why don't we go visit this Bamber person? We can pretend to take him flowers. Or a fruit basket. Then we can get the goods, as the Americans say." Her eyes gleamed with excitement.

"I'm not sure North will let us in to see him," I admitted.

"Are you a woman or a mouse? Forget North! We shall just have to go around him." She stood to her feet. "Grab your hat, Ophelia."

Obediently, I went upstairs. I selected a green cloche to match my shoes and handbag, touched up my lipstick and powder, and went to rejoin my aunt who was nearly trembling with excitement. "Let's go."

It was a rare sunny day so I left the top down. I drove through the streets of London with Butty on my left, hand firmly holding to her hat perched on her gray shingled hair at a jaunty angle. It would have been chic except that it somehow missed the mark entirely and went into the land of ludicrous.

I swung wide around the corner and Butty let out a screech as we nearly plowed into a Royal Mail delivery van. The driver shook a fist at me and shouted something unintelligible. I gave him a smirk and a finger wave.

"The way you drive, it's a wonder you haven't killed anyone, Ophelia."

I ignored her. I drove fine. I was just in a hurry.

Which made me think about the near miss with Alfred Musgrave. That car had been going at quite a clip when it swung toward Musgrave. It had looked like it was on purpose. Had it been? A first attempt on his life that had failed, perhaps. And if so, who was behind it? Which of my many suspects had access to a vehicle and the skill to drive like that? Something to ponder.

I parked out front of the massive gothic building that housed the hospital, and Butty and I hustled inside. Striding to the admissions desk, Aunt Butty demanded loudly, "We're here to see John Bamber."

The nurse behind the desk had a pinched expression as if she was in dire need of prunes in her diet. "I'm sorry, but Mr. Bamber is not allowed visitors."

"But this is his wife," Aunt Butty declared, indicating me.

I tried to hide my startlement and gave the nurse a wide-eyed look which I hoped conveyed anxiety for my supposed spouse. Instead, the nurse looked me up and down.

"I'll bet."

Nothing could budge her. Not even when Aunt Butty tried to bribe her with a ten-pound note. Which, frankly, I considered excessive.

"Fine. We shall leave, but we will be back," Aunt Butty declared. The nurse just gave her an exasperated look. My aunt grabbed me by the arm and steered me outside.

"Now what?" I said. "You let the whole floor know our plan. They'll be looking for us."

"Hardly," she tutted. "There must be a dozen ways into this monstrosity."

"And how do we find Bamber once we're in there?"

She grinned. "I just happened to see his name on the patient list. He's in the East Wing, ward 2A, bed 302."

"How convenient," I said dryly.

"Isn't it just."

We hurried around the side of the hospital toward the East Wing. There were plenty of windows, but the sills were at head height and half hidden behind ornamental bushes. There was no way we were getting in that way. Which was something of a relief. I didn't fancy flashing my knickers to the patients and nurses sunning on the lawn.

We finally found a second entrance around a corner. Heavy greenery blocked the narrow door from sight. I was guessing it was an entrance for nurses and doctors, or perhaps tradesmen. I tested the latch. Sure enough, the door swung open easily. Inside was a narrow hall, utilitarian and empty. I waved at Aunt Butty to follow me and we crept inside, trying not to let our heels echo.

On either side of the hall were doors leading into various rooms for exciting things such as storage, cleaning products, and a small kitchen which I could only assume was for nurses and such as there was no way it could provide for the entire hospital. There were no patient rooms in this part of the building. I supposed we needed to go up.

We came to a staircase of the sort one sees in manor houses for the servants. Clutching the railing, I climbed upward, Aunt Butty behind me. She had been the one who wanted this little adventure, yet she seemed awfully keen on sending me up the stairs first.

On the landing was another door with a window that gave a view out into yet another hall. This one was brightly lit with several open doorways on either side.

"It has to be this floor," Aunt Butty said. "The ward began with a two."

I nodded and pushed open the door. We crept into the hall, trying at once to act as if we belonged there and not to let anyone see us.

"There." She pointed to a doorway which had a sign above it that read "Ward 2A."

I carefully peeked inside. The ward was a large, open room with several windows along one wall. There were at least two dozen beds, each with a male patient. Some moaned in pain or delirium. Others slept. Still others sat and chatted with visitors or quietly read newspapers.

At the far end of the room, off to itself, was a bed next to which sat a uniformed policeman. On the bed huddled John Bamber looking pale and wretched.

"There he is," I said softly. "Now what? There are sisters everywhere." Three nurses—sisters—roamed the ward, administering medicines and comfort. Seemed an awful lot for one ward.

"What we need," said Aunt Butty, "is a diversion."

"Oh, Lord, what are you planning?"

"Get ready." She gave me a sly smile before disappearing down the hall. A few moments later there was a loud crash, followed by screaming and shouting.

The sisters and the policeman all rushed from the room, ignoring me as they charged for the noise. With a quiet laugh, I slipped into the room and took the chair next to Bamber's bed.

"Hello, Mr. Bamber." I kept my voice low to avoid being overheard by the others.

John Bamber's eyelids opened and he stared at me a moment. "You're the woman from the club." There was the faintest trace of nasal Cockney in his voice. "The one that's always sticking her nose in."

"That's quite cheeky coming from the man who has embezzled thousands of pounds from his employer," I said archly.

He had the grace to flush. "I didn't mean to. It's just... she asked me to, you know."

"She asked you to skim a few hundred pounds, not thousands." I gave him a stern look. "I think it's time you told me everything."

"Why?" His expression turned mulish. "You're no copper."

"No," I admitted, leaning forward. "But I am friends with Helena Fairfax and what I tell her about our meeting may seal your future fate." Actually, I doubted any such thing. Helena would likely do whatever she wanted regardless of what I said or didn't say, but *he* didn't know that.

"Fine." He heaved a sigh and stared at the ceiling a moment. "Mrs. Fairfax came to me several months ago. She suspected Mr. Musgrave was trying to take over the club, and she needed a way to fight him. Everything she has is wrapped up in that place. Plus, I never liked Musgrave. Not a nice man."

I murmured something encouraging. He was right about Musgrave.

"So I did it. Twenty quid here or there, at first. It was easy to slip it right past Musgrave's nose. And then, well..." He swallowed, his prominent Adam's apple bobbing up and down in his skinny throat. "You see, I owed some people money. Quite a lot, actually, and they were becoming increasingly aggressive. So, I thought, why not take a little for myself? After all, I was risking a great deal skimming for Mrs. Fairfax."

"Understandable," I encouraged him. "But two thousand pounds is a lot."

"I know." He rubbed his forehead. "Things snowballed. I ended up owing more money. I kept meaning to pay it back."

I didn't say so, but I was beginning to suspect Bamber had a gambling problem. "Of course, you did. You're not a bad person," I soothed. "I suppose it was quite a shock when Musgrave wanted to do an audit."

"Terrible shock. I panicked. I didn't know what to do. Mrs. Fairfax assured me all would be well, but..." He shrugged. "I couldn't stop *worrying*, you know. I was so relieved after Musgrave was killed. He would never know what I'd done. But then Mrs. Fairfax decided to continue the audit. No idea why."

I suspected it was because Helena hadn't entirely trusted him. "You knew she'd find out you'd stolen quite a bit more than she knew about," I guessed.

"Yes," he admitted. "I was terrified! I didn't know what to do."

"So you did the only thing you could think of and tried to end it all," I said a bit dramatically.

His eyes widened. "Good gosh, no! I was going to run, you see. I had a little money left over. My plan was to get the money from my hiding place, go home and pack, and take a ferry tonight to France."

"Your hiding place was at the club?" I guessed.

He nodded. "It was easy enough. A false panel in the wall of the dressing room. No one would be suspicious of my coming and going. I'm the manager, after all."

I frowned. "So you went to the dressing room to retrieve the money."

"Yes. But first, I was a bit... overwrought. Shaking. My nerves, you see. They've never been the same since the Great War. I was at Gallipoli."

Good gosh. No wonder he was a mess of nerves. That disaster of a battle had left over one hundred thousand men dead and destroyed Churchill's career. "I'm sorry to hear that. I was a nurse, so I understand a little."

He nodded. "You saw how it was. In any case, I decided to take some of my tonic. I keep a bottle here at the club. Easier than hauling it back and forth with me all the time."

"Quite sensible," I applauded him. "You take a tonic, not powders?"

"But of course."

"Where do you keep it?"

"In my office, next to Mrs. Fairfax's."

I pondered this. "You went there first. Before retrieving your money?"

"Yes."

"Did anyone else know where you kept the tonic?" I asked.

"Nearly everyone, I imagine. Mrs. Fairfax and Mr. Musgrave were both well aware of my war record. They were very kind to take me on and Mrs. Fairfax assured me that I was welcome to take my tonic whenever necessary. In fact, when she was feeling particularly anxious, I would give her some. She was most appreciative."

Now that was interesting. Perhaps that explained Helena's glassy look the day I met her at Harrod's. She'd probably been hitting Bamber's nerve tonic. "Anyone else?"

He frowned. "Mabel, of course. She's been there longer than I and knows just about everything about everyone."

"I'm thinking specifically about the musicians and singers."

"I imagine they might, as well. I mean, gossip runs rampant in such places. Though I don't know that any of them specifically knew where I kept it."

Interesting. Only three people knew for sure where Bamber kept his tonic and one of them was dead. "All right. What happened next?"

"I tucked my tonic in my pocket and snuck into the dressing room to get the money. I began to feel a bit dizzy. I thought perhaps I would lie down for a moment. Then I could collect the money and continue with my plans. The next thing I knew, I was waking up here."

"You never took any powders?"

"Of course not. I find them vile. So bitter."

"And you weren't trying to kill yourself?"

He appeared shocked. "Definitely not! I may not have the strongest constitution, but I had *plans*. I've always wanted to start a little cafe in Paris. Spend my nights drinking good wine and my mornings walking by the Seine." He stared dreamily into space.

"Did you write a note for Helena?" I asked, wondering if the suicide note had been misconstrued either accidentally or deliberately.

"I did. I wanted to apologize, you see. I knew she'd discover the truth, and she was always good to me. I felt I couldn't go without explaining myself."

"Do you remember what you wrote? Was it on a scrap of paper?"

He gave me a funny look. "No. It was a full sheet. I explained everything. That after I helped Mrs. Fairfax, I'd found myself in trouble and had skimmed more than she asked. That I felt guilty about it. That I was sorry."

"That you couldn't go on working at the club, pretending everything was aces."

"Well, yes. Something to that effect."

I leaned forward. "Do you remember exactly what that line said?"

"I believe it was 'I can't go on like this, but I am too much a coward to face the music.'" He flushed crimson. "Then I said I was sorry and signed it. I planned to leave it in her office."

Instead, someone had taken it and ripped out one single line, adding a period to the end to make it look as if he'd tried to kill himself. Obviously, the killer had planned to pin everything on Bamber: Not just the theft of the jazz club's money, but the murder of Alfred Musgrave.

"What did you know about Musgrave's murder?" I asked. "Quickly. It may save your life."

His eyes widened with fright. "I don't know anything."

"Don't lie to me, Mr. Bamber. You must know something, or the killer wouldn't be after you."

He clutched at the blanket, knuckles white and hands shaking. "It was the room. You see, I found Musgrave first. He was already dead, but the room wasn't messed up. Not like it was later. And the pocket watch was in his pocket. I'm certain of it."

Which confirmed my suspicion that the scene had been deliberately set. "What time was that?"

"Five minutes past one. I was scared the killer would come back. So I ran."

Heavy footsteps echoed in the hall. The policeman was returning. Aunt Butty popped her head through the doorway, hat slightly askew, and beckoned me frantically.

I stood quickly. "Thank you Mr. Bamber. You've been most helpful."

"I have?"

I gave him an enigmatic smile and hurried from the room after my aunt. Behind me came the shout of the policeman. I lifted my skirt and ran for the stairwell.

Aunt Butty was a few feet ahead of me, already halfway down the staircase. The heavy thump of police boots sounded from behind as we hit the first landing and continued on our way. I was worried about my aunt as she was huffing and puffing and swearing like a longshoreman.

Finally, we made the ground floor. Unfortunately, our pursuer was so close I could have sworn I could feel his breath on the back of my neck. Hiding seemed like a good idea.

"In here!" I grabbed Aunt Butty's hand and dragged her into the first room with an open door. It was a rather spartan office with only a simple desk, a chair, and a single case of books against one wall. The only place to hide was behind the curtains gracing the window which overlooked the front lawn.

I grabbed one half and jerked it closed and we slipped behind it. Just in time, too. A floorboard in the hall creaked as the policeman paced up and down, searching for his prey. I turned and eyed the window. It was the only way out. The drop to the lawn didn't look too bad. If I could slide it open, we could lower ourselves out and get away with no one the wiser.

The window slid up easily and quietly enough. I stuck my head out. Four or five feet with a small bush to break our fall. I could go first, and then catch my aunt. I signalled Aunt Butty, pointing to the open window, miming that we should use it to escape.

Just then, the heavy tread of the policeman indicated he'd entered the room. My motions became more frantic. Butty shook her head vigorously. So vigorously that one of the wax grapes dislodged from her hat and hit the floor with a soft *plop*. We both stared in horror as it rolled beneath the curtain and out into the room.

"Ah ha!" the policeman boomed.

"Go! Go!" I practically shoved Aunt Butty out the window. She hit the ground, tangled in the bush. I managed to jump out, barely missing her. I hit the grass, the ground beneath still soft from the morning rain. Jumping to my feet, I glanced up at the window to find a red-faced copper staring back at me.

I grabbed Aunt Butty beneath the armpits, heaved her from the bush, and gave her a shove toward the car park. She charged across the lawn, grapes quivering. I noticed a few extra twigs now graced her hat as I ran after her, ignoring the splatters of mud which now decorated the front of my dress.

Shouts echoed behind us as we hit the graveled parking area. We hopped in the car and sped away, spraying rocks everywhere. Just like the movies.

I careened around a corner on two wheels and nearly took out a milk truck. Aunt Butty gripped the door handle with one hand while holding onto her hat for dear life with the other. We hit the main road and I breathed a sigh of relief. "That was a close one."

"They would have thrown us in prison for sure!" Aunt Butty declared.

I seriously doubted that, but I left her to her wild imaginings and focused on the road. Fortunately, there wasn't much traffic, which meant we sailed along at a good pace.

Aunt Butty glanced behind us and let out a gasp. "I think someone's following us!"

I craned my neck. Sure enough, a car barreled along the road behind us. A very familiar Morris Minor. My heart kicked into high gear, pounding so hard I saw spots dancing in front of my eyes.

I pressed down on the accelerator and the Roadster sped up a little. We roared past genteel houses with white pillars and neat porticos. Nannies walking their charges in prams paused to stare. A small dog on a leash yipped at us, his owner chiding him. A uniformed beat copper shouted and blew his whistle. We ignored him and carried on.

Behind us, the Morris Minor crept closer. Not close enough I could see the driver's face, but enough I could make out a few details of his clothing. He wore a distinctive yellow and green tweed fedora hat. It was Leo Fairfax, the same man who'd run over Alfred Musgrave. I was sure of it! I had a bad, bad feeling. Was he trying to kill us to prevent us revealing the truth about Bamber? Or perhaps because I witnessed what I now realized was no accident, but the attempted murder of Alfred Musgrave?

Pressing harder on the accelerator, the Roadster leapt forward. I whipped around another corner with a screech of tires. Aunt Butty let out a shriek and clasped her bosom. I swerved around another vehicle going much too slow, nearly plowing into a rag and bone cart clopping the other direction. I veered back into my lane just in time to avoid a head-on collision.

"We're going to die!" Aunt Butty wailed.

"Nonsense," I snapped. "Stiffen your spine, Aunt!"

A quick glance in the rearview mirror revealed the Minor hadn't rounded the corner yet. Now would be a good time to hide. But how to hide a car like mine?

Up ahead, I saw a narrow alley. Hoping it was wide enough, I whipped into it, and slammed on the breaks. Aunt Butty was nearly unseated, but managed to catch herself in time.

"Have we lost him?"

I glanced back. "You better pray we have."

"Or else?"

My tone was grim. "Or else we may be dead women."

Shéa MacLeod

Chapter 16

We both watched out the back window. I don't
know about Aunt Butty, but my heart felt like it was
lodged somewhere in the middle of my throat. After what
seemed an age, the Morris Minor sailed by. Was it me? Or
was he going slowly, as if looking for something?

"We lost him!" Aunt Butty crowed.

"For now." I waited a few moments, then cautiously
backed out of the alley. The Minor was nowhere to be
seen and we both breathed out shaky sighs of relief.

A quarter of an hour later found us ensconced at a
cozy table at Claridge's with their largest pot of tea and a
tier of finger sandwiches and pastries that would make
the Queen herself weep with envy. We ignored the grand
arches and elegantly coffered ceiling, intent on restoring
ourselves after our adventure.

"What a close call. Almost getting murdered really
takes it out of a person." Aunt Butty selected an egg and
cress.

My heart rate was returning to normal and now I
wasn't so sure we'd been nearly murdered. Perhaps I had
overreacted slightly. Then again, the driver of the Morris
Minor had been following us and I was sure he was the
one who'd tried to run down Musgrave. So, maybe she
wasn't just being dramatic.

"I, for one, am famished." She took a bite of her egg and cress. "Scrumptious. They do know their way around a tea sandwich."

"That's because you dragged us off before we had luncheon." I went straight for the raisin scones. Piling one high with clotted cream shipped over from Devon and fresh berry jam no doubt whipped up in the hotel's kitchen. It was marvelous.

"More important things to do. Who do you think that was chasing us? And why?"

I had a suspicion about the identity of the driver, but I kept it to myself. For now. "Maybe they didn't want us sharing what we learned at the hospital today."

"What *did* you learn from our mark?"

Aunt Butty had been at the pictures again. I managed to avoid an eye roll, but only just. I gave her a quick rundown of everything Mr. Bamber had told me.

"How fascinating," she said. "It gets more interesting all the time. Who do you suppose killed Alfred Musgrave?"

I gave her a blank stare. Her eyes narrowed.

"You have an idea, don't you?"

"Perhaps. But it needs some fleshing out. I'll have to ponder on it a bit more."

She gave me a sly look. "Playing it rather close to the vest, are we?"

I shrugged and popped another bite of scone in my mouth, wondering vaguely if I could steal the chef away. They really were the most marvelous scones.

She smiled proudly. "You remind me of myself sometimes."

I considered that a compliment. "Is that why you saved me?"

She snorted. "You make it sound so dramatic."

"It was, rather."

"You were sixteen. Everything is dramatic at sixteen."

"True," I admitted. "But my father *did* lock me in my room."

"My brother-in-law is a horse's derrière."

I barely refrained from snorting tea up my nose. "That's one way of putting it, darling."

"It's the *only* way of putting it," she said, liberating a rather scrummy looking raspberry tart from the blue and white china tier.

At age sixteen, I'd fallen wildly in love with a local farmhand. As you do when you're young and full of nonsense. It was ridiculously inappropriate, and I was dead certain it was forever and ever amen. My father, being the sympathetic type, locked me in my room with nothing but bread and water until I came to my senses. Possibly the first time in his life he got truly riled by something other than the arrival of the Patels. Goodness knows what it all would have come to if my mother hadn't put her foot down and rung my aunt. Aunt Butty had come flying in like a feather-festooned whirlwind and whisked me away to her townhouse in London.

"I could not allow you to molder away in that ghastly place," she said firmly. "It just was not on."

By "ghastly place" she meant Chipping Poggs— where I no doubt would have ended up an old maid still locked in my father's proverbial dungeon.

"Well, I don't think I've ever properly thanked you for it. So… thank you."

"Pish posh. It's what aunties do. Have a Victoria sponge. They're divine."

I left Aunt Butty on her doorstep, minus a grape or two, and motored off toward home. Once inside, I kicked off my shoes, changed into a clean frock, rang for tea, and sank down on the sofa with a sigh of relief. I was half way through my second cup of Darjeeling when Chaz rang up.

"Darling, why don't you join me tonight at the jazz club?"

"Sounds lovely, Chaz, darling, but I feel the need of a night to myself."

"You've had a year of nights to yourself," he pouted.

"True. But this is for a good cause. I've nearly cracked the case."

"You know who murdered that ghastly Musgrave?"

"I might. But I need to have a think."

"Understood." He sighed heavily. "I'll have to find someone to take pity on me."

"I'm certain you'll find someone." The telephone wasn't the best way to convey my concern, but it needed to be done, albeit carefully. One never knows who is listening in. "But Chaz, perhaps you should skip the Astoria tonight. Go somewhere else."

"Go where, old thing? The Astoria is the most smashing thing happening right now."

"It's just… I talked to Hale. The, um, pianist."

"Oh, did you?" His voice was light and teasing.

How to say it without revealing too much. "He said a certain gentleman is using it to…"

"To what? Spill it, Ophelia."

"Deal in a certain substance. One with which you are intimately familiar." I winced. I hadn't meant to be so blunt.

"And you think I can't control myself?"

Oh, dear. He was angry. "No. I don't think that at all and you know it. What I do think is that it isn't worth putting yourself in the way of danger."

"You're one to talk."

"I'm trying to solve a mu—" Listening ears, I reminded myself. No need to give the telephone operator extra material for gossip. "I'm trying to assist North."

Chaz snorted. "Very well. If it will make you feel better, I'll go to my club tonight. Satisfied?"

Relief flooded me. "Very."

After he rang off, I padded over to the desk and took a notebook and pen from the drawer. Returning to my perch, I began taking notes in between sips of tea.

First, I wrote Musgrave's name in the middle of the paper with a circle around it. Then from the circle I drew lines poking out like spokes on a wheel. At the end of each spoke went the name of a suspect and his or her motive for murdering Musgrave. Frankly, it didn't get me far. I had no new information.

Bamber's comment about the state of the office when he first found Musgrave dead played over and over in my mind. If he told the truth and the office had been unmussed, the watch unbroken, then the killer must have returned and set up the room to look like a fight had taken place and the watch smashed during the fight. But why?

Because the watch *needed* to be smashed. It was the only way to ensure the police knew the exact time of death. And the only reason *that* would be important was that somehow the killer had an alibi for the specific time of twenty minutes past one.

Which, of course, meant that Musgrave likely hadn't been killed at 01:20 at all. No, if Bamber was telling the truth about finding the body at five minutes past, Musgrave had been killed earlier and the watch changed to match the time the killer needed. Frankly, I believed Bamber. He had nothing left to lose.

Right. I tore off my page of suspects, revealing a clean one. I drew a long line across the center of the page horizontally. Then I drew a shorter line vertically part way across and above it wrote:

12:50 – Alfred arrives for audit.

01:00 – Mabel hears a cough.

01:05 - Bamber finds Body. Office Unmussed. Watch fine.

Further along I drew another vertical line and marked it 01:20 along with the notation that the watch indicated this was when the murder happened and that was when I'd heard what I could only assume was the gunshot. I continued on with my time scale, including everyone's whereabouts and when each thing had supposedly taken place, finishing up with Helena finding the body at 01:30.

Finally, I stared at the timescale for a good long time. Slowly, an idea began to coalesce in my mind.

First, I needed to talk to Mabel again. Then I needed Detective Inspector North's assistance, but I had no doubt he'd hang up on me. Or arrest me.

I reached for the phone and dialed Varant. His butler picked up on the third ring. It seemed ages before Varant himself came to the phone.

"Hello?" His voice sounded tinny, but oddly reassuring.

"I need your help."

Shéa MacLeod

Chapter 17

It had taken some convincing on Varant's part, but Detective Inspector North soon gathered together all the players at the club. I was dying for a highball, but as it was before hours, there was no one to mix one up except for Helena, who was rather busy at the moment. And while I may be one to ignore the niceties, there were police officers present who might frown on me helping myself.

Then again, maybe they wouldn't care. I toyed with the idea a bit longer, giving it up eventually. I needed to keep my head.

Chaz and Varant lounged at the bar, seeing as how they were barely peripherals in the investigation. Chaz was the only one who'd been there during the murder, and he had a rock-solid alibi, having been with me at the time. Not to mention he'd had no reason to kill Musgrave. Especially since Musgrave had been wanting to kick out Leo and his opium dealing.

All the singers and musicians—except for Hale Davis—gathered around one of the larger tables, huddling together as if for support. Helena sat alone at a smaller table, smoking a cigarette. Her husband sat at a table nearby looking hungover.

Doctor Eliot and Aunt Butty—dark eyes bright with curiosity—sat at one of the booths. John Bamber, fresh from the hospital and looking like a wilted daisy, sat with them.

I'd told my aunt she didn't need to come, but she'd donned a tulle smothered hat of a peculiar shade of eye-searing blue and insisted. "I've come this far. I'm not about to back down now!"

Hale sat on the steps leading to the stage, elbows braced on knees and hands clasped together. He was deceptively calm, but the heat in his eyes when he looked at me made me feel thick and fumbly. So I did what any sane woman would do in my situation. I ignored him.

Mabel stood in the corner near the backstage exit shifting uncomfortably from foot to foot. She'd removed her apron in deference to the situation, but still wore the colorful kerchief on her head.

"Ladies and gentlemen, if you please." North's booming voice cut through the low hum of voices. Everyone quieted and turned expectant eyes to the policeman. "I've gathered you together today to go over a few final things."

"You've solved it then?" Josette asked. "You know who killed that ghastly Musgrave?"

North nodded to me. "Lady Rample will explain."

Faces turned toward me, expressions of curiosity and confusion rampant. I strolled to the middle of the room and smiled at them, feeling very much like Agatha Christie's detective, Poirot. Only with better fashion sense and a great deal more sex appeal.

"This was such a bizarre murder, right from the beginning. Don't you think?"

There were some murmurs of agreement, some shrugs. Mostly a lot of bafflement.

"You see, I thought it was strange that the very day after Alfred Musgrave was nearly run down by a car on the streets of London, he winds up dead right here at the nightclub he owned with Mrs. Fairfax. And in the middle of a financial audit, too."

"Dashed odd," Chaz agreed.

I gave him a grateful smile and continued. "I also found it very odd that while Helena's office, the crime scene, was a shambles and Musgrave's watch had been smashed at the time of death, Musgrave himself was quite unharmed. There were no scratches or abrasions to indicate he'd been in a struggle. His clothing was completely unrumpled. In fact, he'd been shot in the back of the head. Why the mess? Unless someone staged it?"

Helena's hand clutched her throat. "But why?" Her eyes were wide and guileless. "Was the killer looking for something?"

"Perhaps," I said. "In fact, it wasn't until I saw the scene of Mr. Bamber's near death, and then spoke to him in the hospital, that I realized what was truly going on."

"Near death," Beau scoffed. "Call it what it is. A suicide. Weakling couldn't handle the truth."

John Bamber stared at his table, looking miserable. A high flush stained his cheeks, but he made no protest.

"Actually, you're quite mistaken," I said. "John Bamber did not attempt suicide. In fact, he was nearly murdered himself."

There was gasps and exclamations. "What happened?" "What do you mean?" "We're gonna die!" This last dramatic pronouncement came from Coco. I refrained from rolling my eyes.

"The two of you planned to kill Musgrave, didn't you?" I whirled on Josette and Beau who stared at me with wide eyes. Beau's mouth was drawn in a tight line. Josette looked like she might faint. "When Josette got the blackmail note, you had no choice. Musgrave had to die."

"Ridiculous," Beau snarled.

"Not really. You see, Josette is a fan of mystery novels. Especially those of Agatha Christie." I strode to the side table in front of DI North and picked up the novel I'd found on Josette's dressing table." This is yours, isn't it, Josette?" I held it up so everyone could see the lurid cover. It showed a scene not unlike the one I'd discovered when I'd entered Helena's office to find Musgrave dead.

"What of it?" Josette demanded, face a little pale.

"It's all in here. You're entire plan." I tapped the cover before setting the book down. "When I saw it, I knew."

"Don't be daft," Beau snorted.

I merely smiled and picked up the gun. It was a surprisingly heavy little thing, cold to the touch. I repressed a shudder and held it up for the room to see.

"This belongs to Beau. There's no doubt about that. He always kept it backstage in his dressing room. He said so. But the night of the murder, he moved it into the planter in Helena's office. You see, I wasn't the only one to hear about the meeting between Musgrave and Helena." I placed the gun back down and turned to face them again. "You knew about it, too," I said to Josette. "You were Musgrave's lover, after all."

"Not out of choice," she bit out.

"No," I agreed, trying not to allow the loathing I had for the victim to overwhelm me. The man was disgusting, and frankly, I wasn't sure he hadn't gotten what he deserved. But still, one couldn't go around killing people simply because they were loathsome. Otherwise there'd be dead bodies the length and breadth of England. "But you knew, and so you planned around it. You would take the gun, use a pillow from Helena's office to muffle the shot, and shoot Musgrave in the head. Then you would hide the gun back in the planter.

"Once you returned to the club, Beau would go back stage and retrieve the gun and set the stage. He would add the time to the note you'd previously collected, smash the pocket watch so the police would think Musgrave died twenty minutes later than he did, and hide the damaged pillow, collecting any loose feathers. Then Beau would go up for a smoke." I turned to face him. "Only instead of smoking out front, you'd sneak around to the back alley and fire the gun next to an open window, timing it for precisely one twenty, when you knew there was a scheduled break in the music. Hopefully, someone would hear it and believe that it was the shot that killed Musgrave. It was all in the book." Once again, I held up the novel. "Except for one small thing: A feather was left behind." I held up the white feather I'd found on the floor of Helena's office the day Musgrave died. North looked apoplectic, but wisely stayed silent.

"Mabel." I turned to face the dresser. "Tell me about the pillow you found. The one with the hole in it."

She blinked and took a hesitant step forward. "I didn't do nothin' wrong, m'lady."

"Of course not," I said bracingly. "Please, just tell us what you found."

She twisted her fingers together nervously. "It were right before the body were found. I was emptying the dust bins and one of 'em had a bunch of feathers in it. Looked in and there was one of madam's pillows. Had a big ole hole in it. Figgured madam had been in a fight with 'er 'usband again."

"What did you do with the pillow, Mabel?" I asked gently.

"Well, it were in the bin, so I took it home. Patched it up. Good enough for me." She crossed her arms with a mulish expression. "I 'ad every right."

"Of course you did," I soothed her. "Tell me, what did this hole look like?"

Mabel shrugged. "Round. Kinda burnt around the edges."

"Bullet hole," North said with utmost confidence. "Someone used it to muffle the shot that killed Alfred Musgrave."

"Except we didn't do it!" Josette wailed. Tears rolled down her cheeks, carrying with them half her eye makeup. Even with her face streaked with black and her eyes red-rimmed, she was stunning. No wonder both Musgrave and Beau had fallen for her.

"No, you didn't." She appeared surprised by my agreement. I continued. "For a long time, I thought it was you. But then I saw something that made me realize someone else wanted Musgrave dead. Someone who'd been cheated and used by him. Someone who wanted the two of you to suffer and so sent the blackmail note to throw us off the scent and frame the two of you."

"Who?" Beau asked.

Instead of answering, I told a story. "A few days ago, I watched Alfred Musgrave nearly get run over by a car. At first it seemed an accident. But then the next day he was murdered. It seemed a stretch that it could be a coincidence. But then I remembered I'd seen something that made me realize it wasn't. Not at all."

"What did you see?" Aunt Butty asked breathlessly.

I turned slowly to face Leo Fairfax. "I saw Mr. Fairfax driving the car that ran over Musgrave."

"Nonsense," Leo sputtered, puffing out his chest. It would have been more impressive if he hadn't been a rumpled mess. It looked like he'd slept in his jacket. Probably had.

"Not at all," I said calmly. "You see, I was able to catch a glimpse of the person driving the car. I could tell it was a man, but I couldn't see his face. I could, however, see his very distinctive fedora hat. The one I saw you later wearing at the club."

"Why would I try and run over Musgrave?" he demanded, cheeks turning red. His eyes darted left and right as if looking for an escape.

"A lot of reasons. He was sleeping with your wife. He was trying to take away your meal ticket. He was a generally unpleasant individual. But the real reason was, Helena told you to."

"Why would I do that, darling?" Helena drawled.

I turned to face her. She stared back at me coolly, smoking her cigarette as if nothing at all were the matter, but I could feel the tension roiling off her. "The same reason you told him to run me and my aunt off the road."

"I did no such thing!" Leo shouted, half standing. North took a step toward him and Leo plopped back down mutter, "I didn't."

"Of course, you did," Aunt Butty said. "Right outside the hospital the other day. You chased us right down the road. We saw you."

Leo snorted. "I wasn't chasing you, daft old woman. I was... visiting a friend and happened to be driving back home."

"Who are you calling a 'daft old woman?'" Aunt Butty snapped.

"Visiting a friend, my ass," Chaz muttered. "More like making a delivery."

So, the incident with the Morris Minor had been all in our heads, after all. I felt a twinge of embarrassment for my overreaction.

"You still haven't answered the question, *Lady* Rample," Helena said. "Why would I have my idiot husband run over my business partner?"

"Because you wanted Afred Musgrave dead. And when Leo couldn't make it happen, you took matters into your own hands."

"Don't be daft, darling," Helena drawled. "Why would I want to off that troll?"

"Because Musgrave wanted to control the club. That was what the audit was about. He suspected that John Bamber was helping you skim money and doctor the books. He was going to use that to force you out."

"Everything I have is in that club. There's no way he was going to get rid of me, whatever he thought." Her tone was angry, bitter. "Doesn't mean I killed him."

"But it does. First you roped Mr. Fairfax into helping you. You arranged to meet Musgrave, then had Leo waiting around the corner. When Musgrave stepped into the street, Leo tried to run him down. But it didn't work, so you had to try something else. Lucky for you, you overheard Beau and Josette's plans. You knew what they were going to do. Or at least you heard the part about shooting Musgrave. You saw an opportunity to get rid of not only the man who threatened to take everything, but the woman who was your sexual rival."

Helena took a deep drag on her cigarette, glaring at me from beneath slitted lids. "And how would I do that?"

"You found the gun first. Sitting in the planter, waiting for you. At one in the morning, you used it just as Josette planned to do and shot Musgrave in the back of the head, using the pillow in your office to muffle the shot. You cleaned up the feathers and ditched them and the damaged pillow in one of the dust bins. You had no way of knowing that Mabel would rescue it from the bin, or that I would find the one feather you missed. When Josette went backstage, she found Musgrave already dead. But what you didn't realize was that Josette and Beau had a plan to save themselves. The two of them were forced to continue the charade of covering up the time of the murder, thus accidentally giving you an alibi along with themselves."

"She's right," Josette whispered. "He was already dead when I went backstage. I was shocked. I didn't know what to do. So I left everything as it was and hurried to tell Beau."

Beau nodded. "That's right. I had to stick to the plan. It was the only thing I could think to do. I was sure the police would pin it on us. And we *had* planned to kill him."

"You can prove nothing," Helena snarled. "Are you going to believe these people over me? They just confessed plotting to murder Alfred."

"But you confessed to an affair with Musgrave," I pointed out. "One that served you very well until Josette came along. Only you had both the motive to kill Musgrave and the motive to pin it on Josette. Plus, only you could have talked Leo into attempted murder."

"Still, you haven't got proof." She lifted her nose, arrogantly certain that she was in the clear.

"Oh, but I have," I said, just as calmly. "You forget about John Bamber."

Helena rolled her eyes. Most unladylike of her. "What about that weasel?"

John let out a squeak of outrage which we all ignored.

"You knew he was stealing from you," I said, "and you wanted to get rid of him. After your original plan failed and Josette and Beau were cleared, you saw your chance. Not only could you get rid of him, but you could pin Musgrave's murder on him. Who wouldn't believe that an embezzler would kill the man about to find him out? Then, overcome with remorse and guilt, kill himself? It was perfect."

"Obviously not," Helena ground out.

"No. Not quite," I agreed. "You see, by poisoning him in the club, he was found too quickly. And thanks to Dr. Elis's quick thinking, his life was spared."

Doctor Elis preened. Helena snarled. She stubbed her cigarette out in the crystal ashtray, smashing it viciously.

"This allowed me the opportunity to talk to Mr. Bamber," I continued. "What I discovered was quite interesting. I'd been very curious about the so-called suicide note. A cryptic line written on a scrap of paper? This didn't at all fit with the man I'd met. So I spoke to him. Not only did he explain that the note had been a line from a much longer letter, but he told me about the nerve tonic which he secretly takes. The tonic only *you* and Musgrave knew about." I pointed dramatically at Helena.

"I don't know what you're talking about," she said.

"Yes, you do. John Bamber told me that he often gave you some of his tonic. Isn't that right, Mr. Bamber?"

"Y-yes," he stammered. "Sorry, Mrs. Fairfax." He shrugged helplessly and sunk lower in his seat.

"So what?" She crossed her arms. "What does that prove?"

"Since you were the only living person who knew about the bottle of tonic Mr. Bamber kept at the club, and his habit of drinking from it when stressed, you were the only one with the opportunity to poison the tonic."

"But he took sleeping powders," she said.

"No, those wrappers were left as mere staging. Mr. Bamber was very clear that he only ever took the tonic. He doesn't care for sleeping powders. Finds them bitter."

"That's right," John Bamber spoke up at last. "I never took any powders."

"Once he'd fallen unconscious, you spread the empty papers about and left the scrap of paper you'd conveniently torn from a letter he'd written you. It was a devious plan," I admitted, "but it didn't quite work."

"Leonard Fairfax, you're under arrest for the attempted murder of Alfred Musgrave." North held up a pair of handcuffs that gleamed dully in the light.

Leo jumped up, face red, stabbing a finger in Helena's direction. "That bitch made me do it! It's *her* fault!" A uniformed officer rushed toward him, slapping the cuffs on his wrists, and dragged him from the room.

"Helena Fairfax," North intoned, "I'm arresting you for the murder of Alfred Musgrave and the attempted murder of John Bamber."

With a screech, Helena leapt from her chair and ran for the door. Chaz made a grab for her and missed. Everyone else sat about stunned, except for Aunt Butty. Aunt Butty calmly stuck her foot out. Helena tripped and went flying... right into the arms of Detective Inspector North.

Shéa MacLeod

Chapter 18

Later that evening, we gathered in Aunt Butty's sitting room. She'd insisted that we all—all being myself, Varant, Chaz, and Hale—come over for drinkies and a natter. No one had dared refuse—one simply didn't tell Aunt Butty no—except for Hale who had insisted his fellow musicians needed him. I kept a stiff upper lip and pretended I didn't feel a stab of disappointment at not being able to spend more time with him. That our steamy evening was destined to remain a one-off. I wondered if, and when, I'd see him again. There'd been talk of the entire group heading to France, or possibly returning to America, now that the Astoria Club was closed. Likely permanently.

He had, however, pulled me to the side, out of sight of the others, after North had marched Helena and Leo out of the club. "Just in case," he'd whispered. Then he'd leaned down and kissed me thoroughly before leaving with his bandmates. It had taken me some time to recover.

I was surprised the police hadn't arrested John Bamber, too, but apparently with one club owner dead and the other arrested for murder, there was no one left to press charges. It was up to whomever inherited the club. No doubt Helena's husband, Leo, although he had his own set of problems what with the failed attempt on

Musgrave's life and his little drugs smuggling business. I still wasn't entirely convinced he hadn't been following Aunt Butty and me with evil intent, no matter what he claimed. And I was relieved to know he'd be gone and away from Chaz for a very long time.

Poor Mabel had been forced to give up her newly mended pillow as evidence. North had been surprisingly kind to her and promised to return it immediately after the trial. That seemed to mollify her. I was more concerned with her immediate welfare, seeing as how she was now out of a job. Aunt Butty rectified that by convincing her friend, Louise Pennyfather, to hire Mabel as her personal lady's maid. I couldn't wait to see how that turned out.

North had given Josette and Beau a strong talking to, but they'd done nothing illegal, technically, unless you counted messing with the crime scene. North seemed happy enough just to get rid of them and call it a night. They appeared harmless enough. Although I wouldn't put it past them to bump off someone in the future should they feel the need. I wondered how long they'd last, or if Beau would go running back to Coco. I was betting on the latter. According to Aunt Butty, leopards don't change their spots.

"How did you ever think to look for that pillow, Ophelia?" Aunt Butty said as Mr. Singh brought in a round of drinks which no one refused. "I daresay I'd have never come up with it."

"Where else would the feather have come from?" I asked. "It wasn't from a hat or a feather boa, so that only left a pillow. And it made sense when Mabel said she heard a cough. No one else heard anything at that time, and yet that had to have been when Musgrave was shot. And while there were pillows everywhere, the one seat in the place that should have had one, didn't. So…it was obvious."

"Well, doesn't that just take the biscuit," Aunt Butty said after gulping back a rather large glass of sweet sherry which Mr. Singh quickly refilled before placing the crystal decanter on the side table and moving away like a silent shadow. "What an adventure this has been. Danger at every turn!"

"Hardly that," Varant murmured, crossing one leg neatly over the other.

Aunt Butty ignored him. "Ophelia and I were practically arrested, chased by a lunatic, sneered at by a police detective. I wouldn't have been surprised if we'd been murdered in our beds!"

Did I mention my aunt can be a tad over-dramatic? No one had been going to murder us, and North had never once sneered at her. Me, on the other hand, he'd been fond of sneering at.

"I'm glad it all came out all right in the end," Chaz said heartily. "It really is too bad the Astoria Club is closed now. Such an entertaining place."

"Where *will* you find amusement?" Varant asked dryly, taking a sip of his sherry.

Chaz waggled his eyebrows. "I've heard of a new place. Very underground. Very hush-hush." He turned to me. "Darling, get your dancing togs. We *must* check it out."

Aunt Butty grabbed the decanter and poured herself more sherry. "Oh, dear. Here we go again."

The End.

Coming in 2018

Lady Rample Finds A Clue
Lady Rample Mysteries: Book Two

Sign up for updates on Lady Rample:
https://www.subscribepage.com/cozymystery

Note from the Author

Thank you for reading. If you enjoyed this book, I'd appreciate it if you'd help others find it so they can enjoy it too.

- Lend it: This e-book is lending-enabled, so feel free to share it with your friends, readers' groups, and discussion boards.

- Review it: Let other potential readers know what you liked or didn't like about the story.

- Sign Up: Join in on the fun on Shéa's email list: https://www.subscribepage.com/cozymystery

Book updates can be found at www.sheamacleod.com

Shéa MacLeod

About Shéa MacLeod

Shéa MacLeod is the author of the bestselling paranormal series, Sunwalker Saga, as well as the award nominated cozy mystery series Viola Roberts Cozy Mysteries. She has dreamed of writing novels since before she could hold a crayon. She totally blames her mother.

She resides in the leafy green hills outside Portland, Oregon where she indulges in her fondness for strong coffee, Ancient Aliens reruns, lemon curd, and dragons. She can usually be found at her desk dreaming of ways to kill people (or vampires). Fictionally speaking, of course.

Shéa MacLeod

Other Books by Shéa MacLeod

Made in the USA
San Bernardino, CA
15 December 2018